THE DELIVERY

THE DELIVERY

PETER MENDELSUND

FARRAR, STRAUS AND GIROUX

NEW YORK

Farrar, Straus and Giroux
120 Broadway, New York 10271

Printed in the United States of America
First edition, 2021

Library of Congress Cataloging-in-Publication Data
Names: Mendelsund, Peter, 1968– author.
Title: The delivery / Peter Mendelsund.
Description: First edition. | New York : Farrar, Straus and Giroux, 2021.
Identifiers: LCCN 2020042799 | ISBN 9780374600426 (hardcover)
Classification: LCC PS3613.E48223 D45 2021 | DDC 813/.6—dc23
LC record available at https://lccn.loc.gov/2020042799

Our books may be purchased in bulk for promotional, educational,
or business use. Please contact your local bookseller or the Macmillan
Corporate and Premium Sales Department at 1-800-221-7945, extension
5442, or by email at MacmillanSpecialMarkets@macmillan.com.

www.fsgbooks.com
www.twitter.com/fsgbooks • www.facebook.com/fsgbooks

1   3   5   7   9   10   8   6   4   2

To Henoch and Shiffra, who never went home

PART I

Our language can be seen as an ancient city:
a maze of little streets and squares, of old and
new houses, and of houses with additions from
various periods; and this surrounded by a
multitude of new boroughs with straight
regular streets . . .

CHAPTER ONE

Delivery 1: ★★

CHAPTER TWO

It was raining, lightly. The wheels of the bicycle hissed down the streets.

———————

Customer two had smiled, and said something to him he hadn't entirely understood. She looked the delivery boy briefly in his eyes, before closing the door.

CHAPTER THREE

"She said to 'stay dry.'"

"A manner of speaking," N. said, not turning away from the dispatch computer, in case the Supervisor saw them talking.

Little-to-no traffic. Few customers.

(Slow time.)

The rain let up.

CHAPTER FOUR

(N. taught him. *Customer, block, delivery, doorman, side-walk, elevator, manor house, tenant, stoop, Supervisor, "stay dry,"* so on.)

CHAPTER FIVE

Third delivery.

———————

An indifferent man; a customary tip.

———————

(No stars.)

———————

The sun came out. Having rolled up his sleeves at a traffic light, the delivery boy felt the hairs on his forearm ruffle.

———————

Slow, slow. The delivery boy squinted.
     Still early, though.

———————

Slow times were

    1. Bad: few tips, but also

    2. Good: no rushing or poor ratings.

——— —

He stopped at another light, listed over onto one foot, looked right, left.

———

Where were the customers. Maybe it was a holiday?

———

(Holidays were slow times . . .)

CHAPTER SIX

Green awnings (stippled from the rain).

Manhole covers (latticed).

Trees (on the median. Marbling shadows).

Pedal; coast. Pedal; coast.

Light (strobing).

The smell of the hot, wet pavement.

The phone: heavy in his pocket.

CHAPTER SEVEN

The holidays here were different from the ones back home.

———————

Though he did not know all the names of the months and seasons, he had heard from N. about one or two of the local holidays.

———————

(When they were, how they were observed . . . etc.)

———————

There was a backfire. Someone shouted. A bus pulled into his lane.

———————

The delivery boy drove around the bus, not knowing for a moment what lay on the far side.

———————

"You can still do our holidays," N. had allowed, with that weary look of hers.

———————

Adding hastily, as he walked away toward the store-room door: "in private!"

———————

The light turned green, but he had kicked off just before, knowing the rhythms of the lights, and of everything on the street.

———————

Later, he had said:
"We should try their holidays."
"Don't be stupid."

CHAPTER EIGHT

Fourth customer: ★

———————

Customer four was in a hurry.

The man had spun away from the delivery boy almost as soon as he took the parcel. In the customer's haste, the hand of the delivery boy and the hand of the customer had touched.

———————

"Do not touch the customer."

(N. was right, of course, but still it happened.)

———————

When the delivery boy's hand accidentally brushed the knuckles of a nervous, old, or overquick customer, he received poor tips, and was given: no stars; no stars; one star. (Respectively.)

"Coming through."

Back at the warehouse, he checked the numbers, and then the tall shelves: two light shopping bags and two medium-size boxes.

The bags had gone over the handlebars, one box went under his left arm, the second was bungeed to the rack.

He had four bungees: two red, a yellow, and a green.

(The fifth customer had given him five stars and a 30 percent tip on a very large order.)

The sixth customer had smiled also, in the manner of the lady earlier, and had tipped him generously.

———————

The bungees had been handed out to the delivery boy—along with his helmet and phone—by the shelf manager. The shelf manager was known by everyone as "Uncle," and he was old and lank, with hard eyes. Uncle's fingertips were yellow.

———————

There had been strict instructions concerning all items belonging to the warehouse, which the delivery boy had understood in only the most general sense.

———————

Seventh customer: average-to-big-size tip.

———————

The day was improving. Even with average stars, the tips were piling in.

———————

(Piling *up*.)

    "Right," he said to himself, remembering.

The delivery boy coasted downhill on a road that bordered a little park. The trees and the road curved and sloped downward, gently, in unison.

Honk.

    "Fucker!"

(The general sense of the warehouse instructions had been—through a haze of missed words and half-understood phrases—that the phone and helmet and bungees and bicycle all belonged unequivocally to the warehouse.)

He leaned forward, down the hill.

The park and the road.

———————

(These things belonged to the warehouse. Everything did.)

———————

The delivery boy, looking over his shoulder, back up to the crest behind him, felt an unexpected tenderness, having noted the bend of the park and the road.

———————

It would be a very hot day.

———————

(The choreography implicit in the setting, the way the park and the road had curved—or perhaps it was the swaying of the trees—reminded the delivery boy of the dances; like those held in his homeland, on the marble floor of the old public hall.)

———————

The feeling aroused in the delivery boy was (to my surprise) a form of pity.

———————

The delivery boy, as a rule, had not participated in these dances.

———————

The music had made him queasy; the accumulation of perfume, aftershave, and sweat had made him queasy; the marble dance floor's lack of friction had made him queasy . . . But, mostly, his queasiness was due to not knowing the rules that governed partnership; i.e., who danced with whom, and why.

———————

He wore a jacket to the dances. Which had seemed proper.

(The girls: ankle-length dresses.)

———————

The delivery boy flipped up his visor, wiped the back of his hand across his forehead.

———————

Customer eight. Pickup at a corner café.

———————

(Or perhaps it wasn't the curve in the road, or the trees; but it might have been the swish of a skirt of a girl on the street that reminded him of the dances. Anyway.)

———————

The delivery boy waited in the short line, and when he reached the counter, he held out the receipt and waited.

———————

The girl behind the counter had such slender wrists.

———————

He handed over the order form, and did not speak.

CHAPTER NINE

As he cruised down a hill, the delivery boy reached under his seat and flicked off the bicycle's power-assist.

———————

The sky lightened.

———————

If the sun came out, he figured, the girls would come out too.

———————

Customer nine: decent tip, no comments. ★★★★

———————

Comments, if they were good, were the best for a delivery boy's average and his prospects.

———————

The Supervisor took you into the office with the barred door if he became aware of negative comments.

———————

At the very bottom of the rise, the delivery boy had stopped at a light, in a spot where the branches formed a generous awning. While straddling the bike, he pulled out his water bottle and took a long slug. He followed the water's cooling passage down the inside of his chest until it leveled out at his midriff. He burped. Checked his phone.

———————

Ahead.

———————

It was slow, and he was ahead.

———————

So he breathed deeply, twice, then he pushed off again, coasted to the curb, threw a leg over the bicycle, laid it down gently on the sidewalk, and sat on the sidewalk, his feet on either side of a small storm drain.

The delivery boy had seen a dispatch girl come out of the Supervisor's office, only days earlier. She had a hand clamped over one side of her face, as if testing the vision in her other eye.

Never mind.

The day continued to warm.

Here and there, the old, used-up rain had collected, and was running into drains, carrying stuff—leaves, sticks, and some of the little yellow blossoms from the park trees—small bits of garbage. There was also a plastic glove, some cigarette butts, and a magazine that was stuck to the side of the grate. The magazine was missing half of its cover, and was slowly being turned into a colorful pulp. He looked up, away from it, and watched the water streaming down the edge of the curving hill; watched the debris carried along down this shining ribbon, drawn toward his feet.

———————

Checked his phone again.

———————

It would get absurdly hot, if it didn't rain again.

———————

But the girls would come.

———————

Surely.

———————

And he could look.

———————

Only look.

———————————

(Not knowing the rules that governed . . .)

———————————

And the day heated up further, but the sky was still overcast. (I imagine the leaves were that pale green you often see before a storm.)

So the streets remained fairly empty.

———————————

The trees were almost glowing (such was the quality of this pale green color).

———————————

It would pass over quickly, he decided, and checked his phone once more.

———————————

He considered N., who had not messaged him for some time.

It is either a very slow day for her, or else she is very busy, he reasoned, concluding, jealously, that some of the other delivery boys must be doing quite well.

He prodded the shallow stream with the tip of his shoe, making it, briefly, two streams.

CHAPTER TEN

N. gave him the promising jobs.

———————

But when he first arrived—before he and N. had spoken to each other, so on—every day was a slow day.

———————

Moving packages from one warehouse to another. No customers. No tips, no comments. He was *barely better than Wodge*.

———————

No better than his own bicycle.

———————

Then N. worked something out. He was promoted.

———————

The delivery boy didn't understand (her benevolence toward him).

———————

Maybe he reminded her of someone? Whatever.

———————

But things improved, then.

———————

Still, he remembered that, even after, there were periods when the rate of his pickups and deliveries would slow.

———————

1. When he had pressed her about them doing the new holidays, or
2. When he had lost or forgotten tip money, or
3. Didn't get required signatures, or
4. The time he had asked her about her parents, or
5. Just when he spoke to her too frequently, or
6. Spoke to her in front of the other dispatch girls. Such periods.

———————

(Which is to say that the delivery boy knew: that she was speaking to him through the dispatches themselves.)

———————

Cars and buses went by as he sat.

———————

They went by, and by, until they formed a kind of fuzzy wall in his mind. There was that scent of wet grass. Sweet and rotten. (And the charcoal scent of wet pavement.)

———————

There had been a park on a trip with his youth orchestra—in a country next to his own. In the park was a carnival, with rides, and a beautiful gazebo.

———————

The conductor of the youth orchestra (the delivery boy remembered him, then). The conductor's coat had been yellow.

The delivery boy's plastic lighter was also yellow.

    He shook it up and down.

The delivery boy lit a stub. He rounded his spine backward, until he was leaning on his elbows.

"This is the best week here," N. said, the night before, as he handed over his tips in the warehouse hallway. Everyone was in the bunk room.

The Supervisor had been away. She was looser. More relaxed.

"A great week. The yellow trees flower only once a year," she continued. "It is superpretty. Though it will only last five, six days, tops."

———————

"After that, do the blooms all fall down at once?"

"Gah, yes; and then they smell like vomit."

———————

(This, for N., passed as expansive.)

———————

Buzz.

———————

The delivery boy looked at the small, dirty stream. His phone buzzed, and buzzed again, and he hoiked himself up and threw his leg over his power-assist bicycle. He leaned on the handlebars, wrapped tightly with plastic bags. He waited for an opening between cars, and then kicked off, expertly.

———————

Customer ten.

CHAPTER ELEVEN

Customer eleven. (Doorman building.)

––––––––––––

"Doormen," N. repeated sourly. "Superintendents, guards, concierges . . ."

"Concierges."

"Old women. Who live in little rooms, off of the courtyards."

"Ah."

––––––––––––

"You can always maneuver through heavy traffic," she explained, "but if somebody decides that you should wait for a service elevator, or worse still, shouldn't be in the building at all . . ."

––––––––––––

There was—though only once—a town house.

Almost all the grand houses were—according to

N.—uptown, to the north; across the river in Manor Grove. This one was relatively modest, the only one in its neighborhood (so, perhaps a vestige of an older, different city). It had neither a concierge nor a doorman, but rather a manservant in a cutaway coat. The manservant was startled and displeased to see the delivery boy, who had been whisked around to a back stairwell. (Manor houses have their own, dedicated delivery boys.)

The delivery boy had suspected that going up to the front door of this type of building wasn't correct, but hadn't heeded these qualms, and so had been told off.

(That is to say: no matter how much N. explained to him, and how carefully he listened, there were always cases that were not covered in the lessons.)

(And, though the delivery boy's and N.'s languages were similar—their homelands adjacent—there were inevitable mistranslations, and every variety of awkwardness.)

———

This next delivery (customer eleven) was to a normal building though, with a customary doorman, who was half seated on the lip of his high stool, leaning the (brocaded) upper part of his heavy frame on a desk. He barely acknowledged the delivery boy, just shrugged him on past, in a weary, practiced manner.

———

"Hey—"

As the delivery boy was about to enter the elevator, he was called back. Could he take an envelope up with the food? The delivery boy nodded. The doorman handed the envelope to him (his epaulets barely stirring).

———

It was almost always the case that doormen had him do the deliveries himself, directly to the customer's door— though occasionally it was the policy that all packages be left downstairs. When this was the case, there would be no tip.

———

N. never sent the delivery boy to such buildings. Not unless he was annoying her, anyway.

———————

The delivery boy made sure not to smudge the envelope with the grease from his power-assist bicycle.

———————

The elevator was one of those small, clear ones that rise through the center of a central stairway; its door folding like an accordion.

At every floor he passed, there was a small, flat sound.

———————

Baaaah.

———————

The delivery boy stepped out onto the floor and was greeted by customer number eleven.

———————

Customer eleven was very excited to see the envelope the delivery boy held out to her. So much so that the delivery boy had thought then, for a moment, that she, the customer, in her exuberance, would embrace him. Instead, she snatched up the doorman's envelope without giving any attention at all to the bag in the delivery boy's other hand.

Envelope creasing in her tight fist, she spun around and disappeared into her flat.

The door followed on her heels like a dog.

(Slam.)

The delivery boy felt, at that moment—

The door reopened.

"Silly me!"

Her hand shot out.

She put the food down just inside the threshold of the apartment, fumbled in her robe for a moment, and handed the delivery boy his tip before rapidly closing the door a second time.

He stuffed the bills into his pocket without counting them—and it was only after he was downstairs that he realized how much he had made.

The delivery boy had also been granted a slight glimpse of customer eleven's bare legs.

_____

(Things were going, he thought, with not a little bit of pride: *pretty good.*)

_____

Back at the bike, he slung the chain over his head. Before kicking off, he took a moment to rub the bills between his fingers, enjoying their raggy suppleness.

_____

"Look," he pinged to N., beneath a snap of the money, piled up on his palm.

CHAPTER TWELVE

Customer twelve: one star. Low, low tip. Bad.

"Coc-ky."

This was several months back, on his first big-time day.

Late, late night, when he had locked off the power-assist bike for good, and come into the dispatch corridor with his haul, N. had reached for his device and the receipts, rubber-banded to it. Usual procedure.

Just as her fingertips touched it, he snatched it back, rapidly.

"Uh-uh," he chided her. *Come and get it.*

"Don't be cocky."

"What."

"It means thinking you are hot shit."

He didn't know what she meant, so grinned, stupidly.

Back at the warehouse.

Locked his bike.

Went straight to the package room.

"Coming through."

("Coming through" is what delivery boys say as they push through large swinging doors. They say this so as not to hit someone on the other side. They all observe this protocol. The Supervisor never said anything when he came through the door though—quiet as a scorpion—and it was, generally speaking, habitual for all of them to not only shout, but to look and listen carefully before entering the hallway. No one wanted to barge into the Supervisor. Forgetting this could come at a great cost.)

No one was in the hallway.

———————

In the warehouse, Uncle sat in his low-slung chair, glaring at the delivery boy. He slowly rolled a cigarette, without looking down at it.

———————

The delivery boy searched the tall shelves for his next deliveries (K332, W520 . . .), and when he had them in hand, he marked them all down on the clipboard, writing slowly and carefully. (It was Uncle's job to check these, which he did assiduously.) The delivery boy sped through the dispatch corridor, and was out again.

———————

As he approached the stand of bicycles, the delivery boy could have sworn that one of the wrapped boxes he carried had shuddered.

———————

(As a rule, the delivery boy did not know what it was that he was delivering.)

———————

Several blocks on, while he was coasting down a long thoroughfare, the package shuddered again, on his rack.

———————

(He did not know what he delivered, but had guesses, of course. And sometimes the identity of the pickup location—if the pickup location wasn't the warehouse, that is—would be a sure indicator. Bakery, newspaper stand, dry cleaner, etc.)

———————

(Also some deliveries were, quite obviously: what they were. 1. Food [smell]. 2. Papers [envelope]. 3. Bowling ball [shape, weight . . .]).

———————

When he stopped then to retighten the bungees (one yellow, one red) only then did he notice the discreet air holes cut into the sides of the wrapping paper.

———————

(For the most part though, the contents of the packages he delivered remained private.)

He locked the bike, hefted the box with the air holes cut in it, pushed the buzzer's worn brass nubbin, and went up.

Two children answered the door. Each child took one side of the box, though it wasn't heavy.

Their eyes did not waver from the delivery boy's face as they accepted the delivery, despite a small, yet discernible, scrabbling sound coming from inside of it.

The delivery boy looked at the box held in common by these solemn children, and raised one eyebrow at it, showily. Then looked back at the children.

They seemed then, if anything, to become even more grave, to sink deeper into themselves, and backed up, feeling their way with bare feet.

The father moved in then, did the tip, so on.

But after: muffled sounds of glee.

———

The delivery boy, back on the street, looked at his lock-screen, clicked the phone off again, and mounted up.

———

Two more (average-to-good) deliveries.

———

In and out.

———

(The delivery boy had owned a pet once.)

———

(A turtle. Or a . . . cat.)

CHAPTER THIRTEEN

There was nothing else in this lobby besides the door-man in his chair, and the enormous fan.

———————

(As if the lobby were being used to assess doorman-aerodynamics.)

———————

The delivery boy had not realized how hot it was until he saw the fan. Noticing it, he felt the heat moving on the breeze.

———————

There was no elevator, so the delivery boy walked up the four flights to customer sixteen.

———————

Some apartment doors open silently. When a door opened silently, it meant that the customer had been waiting behind the door—a door that, in fact, was already open, but only looked closed. The customer, in these cases, would be 1. Hungry. 2. Anxious. 3. Unemployed. (Their eyes pressed to tin bezels, eager hands on knobs, listening for telltale sounds . . .)

———————

Most doors opened after a small turning sound, followed by a large *chunk*.

Some doors opened after several of these *chunk*ing sequences.

———————

On occasion, there was the rattle-slide-rattle of a chain being taken off.

Only twice has there been the sound of a bar being removed.

———————

The Supervisor's door had a bar. The delivery boy had heard the bar being set in place.

The Supervisor's door had a plaque, of yellowish metal, that said SUPERVISOR.

———————

"Don't fuck with him."

———————

She needn't have told him that. (Furthermore, N. had known that her warning wasn't—strictly speaking—needed.)

———————

(Of course the delivery boy already knew that the Supervisor was a fucker.)

———————

He'd seen the Supervisor take people into the office. It was always the same: the worker (warehouse boy, delivery boy, dispatch girl, so on) would go in first, then the Supervisor would look behind him once, briefly, before going in himself and closing the door, and barring it.

―――――――

The Supervisor's gaze was half-lidded.

―――――――

And there was the way—while the Supervisor looked at you (half-lidded)—that he worried a toothpick; the jaw muscles on one side of his mouth throbbing.

―――――――

Strongmen are like this, thought the delivery boy.

―――――――

(And there had been that one time: when the delivery boy had seen the dispatch girl leaving the Supervisor's office . . .)

―――――――

(. . . when the dispatch girl looked up, quick, and had turned her face from the delivery boy, and skittered into the dark.)

―――――――

The delivery boy had tried out the Supervisor's look of dreary menace on his own face, in the bathroom mirror.

———————

Customer sixteen. Good tip, no stars, no comments.

CHAPTER FOURTEEN

He was ahead.

———————

1. Ahead in terms of money. 2. Ahead in terms of time.

———————

He stopped again at a corner shop for more smokes.

———————

Then he stopped again after that, at a little park, no more than the width of two sidewalks. This slender park was at the edge of some large stone steps, which led up to an impressive building. (A mausoleum? Government office? A museum, probably.) People drifted by. Some went in, some came out. The hot afternoon light cast hard, short shadows. He tasted the residue of tobacco in his mouth. The yellow flowers rippled above him—pretty. He thought about the many pictures that must hang in this museum.

———————

(And scenes from his own life: portraits, landscapes, still lifes. A long and narrow private gallery: bright pictures glinting out from the receding dark walls.)

———————

The slow time continued.

———————

(He luxuriated in it.)

———————

He counted ten pictures on the walls of his imaginary gallery.

———————

And grew very calm.

———————

He felt content. As contented, perhaps, as he had ever been in this city.

As contented as he had felt since before the vessel.

———————

The delivery boy remembered a particular picture.

———————

In this picture, the entire world was shown in minia-ture. Fields, mountain ranges, cities: each no more than the shake of a brush. Small daubs were churches and government buildings, homes and markets, and people were little more than dots from the tip of a sharpened pencil. Everything clustered at the banks of this wind-ing, inky-dark river.

———————

N.'s hair.

———————

The river.

———————

(The delivery boy did not think about the vessel.)

He mounted his power-assist bicycle again, but just sat on it for a while. A bus began to pull into his spot, so he pushed out, skillfully, like a skiff on fast water, and was on the go again.

Off, into the flow of traffic.

Today, thought the delivery boy, would be a big-time day.

And the number seventeen is a lucky number in the old country. So the delivery boy just figured . . .

CHAPTER FIFTEEN

The doorman called up, the delivery boy waited, the doorman spoke to the big switchboard, the delivery boy was pointed to the elevator bank on the right.

The customer was on the third floor, so it would all be over in a flash.

The customer could not find his wallet.

Sounds of the customer rooting around (the delivery boy couldn't see very far into the darkened entryway); the seconds and the minutes ticked by, each one counting against the supply the delivery boy had in trust.

Time passed. The seventeenth customer made apologetic noises.

The elevator doors closed behind the delivery boy and left the floor.

———————

There was a device above the elevator that counted the floors. It was semicircular, with an arrow. (Like the top half of a clock.)

———————

The delivery boy stood in the hall as the elevator went down, then up, and then down again, describing a portion of a half circle.

———————

The doors opened. A man and a woman came out. They looked sideways at the delivery boy, and entered their own apartment, latching their door; the kind of door that locks with a heavy click.

———————

The delivery boy waited more. The bank of the delivery boy's time-per-customer diminished further.

———————

The dispatch girls clocked distance-and-time-per-delivery.

———————

The Supervisor would check these figures. Not always, but at random times.

———————

The delivery boy heard a peephole slide open behind him.

He waited, and anticipated hearing it chime closed.

———————

It didn't.

———————

Customer seventeen returned to the hallway and gestured to the delivery boy.

The customer was out of breath. "Better you should wait in here."

"Never go into their homes," N. had warned, with particular emphasis.

But the delivery boy could not stand in the hallway forever; he did not want trouble from the doorman, and he was reluctant to frighten the customer's neighbors any further.

He took a few steps, and just like that he was inside.

Then they went even farther in: leaving the dark vestibule and entering a large room.

Bright, colorful.

———

There were framed pictures on the walls. Clustered on every surface of the room and its furniture were objects (little figurines, fetishes, pieces of art, souvenirs, small easels with photos and miniature paintings, curios made of clay, wood, metal, so on. Dolls, pots, antiques of every stripe. On one of the walls was a large tapestry. Under it, on a wooden column, was a contraption involving thread and wood, a spindle of some sort, but not one that could possibly work in any meaningful way. There was political memorabilia, porcelain busts of old-world leaders, antique toys, and a large, tapering cylinder of brass. Puppets. Trinkets. Books on shelves, and on the floors. Stamped-metal road signs, architectural plans, clocks, a pendulum, a stuffed warbler . . .)

———

"I'm sure it's in the kitchen . . ."

———

The delivery boy loosened the top button of his shirt.
    Cocky, he thought.

———

Time ticked by, but then the delivery boy saw a statu-
ette—of the Strongman, the ruler of the delivery boy's
homeland. It was standing among a crowd of other busts
and junk, as if it were simply another knickknack.

The delivery boy left the bag on the floor of the colorful room.

He closed the front door quietly behind him.

He took the stairs down.

Later, sitting at a red light, he closed his eyes hard.

Stupid, *stupid*.

"That was a cash order," N. reminded him.

("The Strongman" was not the name of the tyrant from
the delivery boy's homeland, but will suffice.)

(Generalissimo, Commissar, General Secretary, Field
Marshal, Chairman . . .)

No. No. The delivery boy was fine.

He was *fine*.

(The dispatch girl who had turned away from the delivery boy in the warehouse corridor: for a week afterward, she had brushed her hair forward, and to the left.)

Yes, he was fine. He would pay for customer seventeen's meal himself. He would pay with the cash tip from customer eleven, which covered half of the cost, and the rest he would pay for out of his tips share.

So.

Customer eighteen.
Average.

"Pull yourself together," N. said.

(N. had no patience.)

Rain again.
Pelting his helmet with mean little beaks.

CHAPTER SIXTEEN

His legs were, like his bicycle, wrapped tightly in plastic delivery bags. These were, in turn, coiled with tape.

There were bags on his feet, covering his sneakers as well.

Another delivery boy had shown him these tricks.

That particular delivery boy had stopped coming to the distribution center . . . was it months ago?

N. thinks this missing delivery boy got a job upriver, in Manor Grove.

———————

The senior delivery boys weren't so sure.

———————

"Who knows," N. pronounced conclusively.

———————

It was hot and wet.

———————

The delivery boy also wore a poncho, made of a large, pale garbage bag.

He saw himself in the bike's mirror.

———————

Garbage ghost. I am a garbage ghost.

———————

The day the delivery boy left his homeland, the town had been covered in a deep snow. There had been several other children from the youth orchestra in the belly of the vessel there, squeezed in next to the delivery boy, all of them craning to see the colorless town recede through a small window.

———————

None of the children had their instruments with them.

———————

Garbage ghost, garbage ghost coming through! the delivery boy shouted (to the rain).

———————

(In his native tongue.)

———————

(In his head.)

———————

It was slippery out. He had to pay proper attention.

———————

And, and . . . something was a bit loose on the power-assist. It was making a small, two-syllable, hollow sound.

Cocky. Cocky, cocky, cocky . . .

As if to confirm his sense of impending bad luck, as he swung right onto a side street, out of nowhere came another power-assist bike, directly across his path.

His brakes sobbed.

Near collision.

"Fucker!" the delivery boy shouted involuntarily, while his mount veered, violently juddered, then righted.

But the other delivery boy had already moved on, out of earshot.

"Fucker," said the delivery boy again, without conviction.

He hopped off the bicycle, picked up the fallen—though barely dented, and still miraculously dry—box. He strapped it back onto the rear rack using the (green) bungee.

———— ————

He sped down the rest of the side street, his bike still clicking, and now also thrumming at a slightly lower pitch.

————————

The delivery boy stopped outside the destination, dismounted, and locked the bike to a signpost. He pulled once, hard, on the chain, to ensure that it was properly wound.

————————

He looked back up the street to the site of the near-accident, then down to his mechanism.

————————

(The person who had almost run over the delivery boy was one of those errand runners who take all their orders directly from customers. The delivery boy could tell, seeing the errand boy's bright red bag.)

———————

A shadow of envy drifted across his features.

———————

What would it be like, the delivery boy wondered (to be clever enough—capable enough—lucky enough to not need a warehouse at all; not need a dispatcher, a Supervisor . . .)

———————

Then came customer nineteen.
Normal tip, no comments.

———————

Green, green, green, green . . .

———————

But he can't rush now, with the damaged mechanism.

The delivery boy's phone buzzed in his pocket once more.

Warehouse.

He strode right by N., as she made no move to speak to him.

(No stars, no comments, he thought gloomily.)

"Coming through."

Parcel numbers B113, G725 . . .

He picked up his next parcels, and headed out once more into a light rain.

Hot and wet. Hot and wet.

———————

Dark and shiny streets. Wheels sluicing through them.

(Smells of metal, exhaust. The city drawn in dust and ash.)

———————

Customer twenty. Food delivery. More food smells.

———————

"*Gro-ss*. It means vomit." N. leaned over with her pointer finger headed to her (cartoonishly) wide-open mouth, pantomiming a big throw-up.

"It means," she continued, "smells bad." Then she pointed to a door.

"Boys shower here. Go."

———————

While on the vessel, the delivery boy had lost his sense of his own body's smell, though it had returned over time.

At one point, he found a mostly used-up bottle of body spray in the bunk-room trash, and used it in small, carefully portioned amounts.

The delivery food in the bag on his handlebars smelled super.

He thought about what would happen if he were to reach in and pinch some out of one of the tiffins. But the light turned green, and once again he kicked off, just as before. Just as skillfully.

(Not that he *would ever.*)

After dropping off the next delivery (customary tip) he clambered up on the bicycle again and drove, at first cautiously, then with more confidence, as the noise from the bike "let up."

———————

(The second rain also "let up.")

———————

He stopped at another median strip, pulled some jerky from his pants pocket, and tugged off a hank.

———————

He put an empty plastic bag down, fastidiously, and sat.

At one point, someone sat on the far side of his bench, then left.

———————

The delivery boy considered the people around him. He flicked his eyes left, right, to the pedestrians on the walkway, going into shops and courtyards, waiting at crosswalks, then to the drivers in their vehicles.

I know when that car is going to pull out, he thought.

"... *now.*"

(And it did.)

So he knew the rhythms of the street, sure. He knew how these people moved. He knew when they moved, and how fast they would move. But he did not know the deeper rules governing the people themselves. Just timings, speeds, so on.

(In other words, he knew when, but not why.)

The delivery boy asked himself:

What does that cap there mean; what does that skirt say; what manner of expression is that; what kind of old man is this?

CHAPTER SEVENTEEN

"Stay dry."

———————

(The delivery boy took it as a rebuke, or an order. But it meant "thank you.")

———————

The day of his first youth orchestra rehearsal, he had noticed several of the violin players—as well as the principal oboe, and the timpanist—had worn small badges on the lapels of their green blazers.

———————

(If it had been merely one person with a badge on his or her lapel, the delivery boy would not have cared so much. But the fact that there had been a group of them . . . This suggested that the badge meant something in particular.)

Eventually the delivery boy asked one of the violinists:

"What is that badge."

"Don't worry about it."

So he tried the timpanist, a scrawny boy who stood next to the delivery boy at the back of the youth orchestra.

"It's the future," the boy said, looking away from the delivery boy with studied nonchalance.

"But why do you wear it?"

The timpanist's expression said that this should have been the most obvious thing in the world.

Then the conductor rapped his baton, and all conversation stopped.

———————

Okay.

So the badge was "the future."

It wasn't much. But even that was information. Of a sort.

(In my experience, any information, at the start, is important. Even a refusal to provide any.)

———————

The delivery boy was beginning to get a sense about which customers would give good tips, for instance.

———————

Not always, only sometimes.

———————

It had occurred to him—when the man he was delivering the package of books to answered the door—that this man would under-tip him.

And the delivery boy had been correct.

———————

Far up ahead on the sidewalk. A woman pushing a baby stroller.

The delivery boy made a small wager with himself.

———————

As his bike sped past the woman, he slowed slightly, craned his neck.

Then he turned back to the road ahead, satisfied.

———————

(The woman's stroller had not contained a baby, but a small dog.)

"Knew it."

(Actually, the delivery boy had guessed "bags," but "dog" was close enough. The important thing was that he had known at a glance that there would be no baby.)

"Five stars for me, fuckers," the delivery boy crowed.

CHAPTER EIGHTEEN

"Hey," the delivery boy said (sub-audibly) to N., as he walked by, waiting just a beat, which he hoped was not noticeable, for a response that did not come, before hustling to—and then through—the wide, swinging door, and into the storage rooms.

———————

"Coming through."

———————

"You'll see."

"I don't know about that."

"Soon they won't need you, or me, or the bikes at all."

"But someone still has to deliver the packages."

"No. Not people."

"How will they get to the customer?"

"Computers, asswipe."

———————

Smoke circled the bulb above the heads of the idle delivery and stock boys.

———————

"Asswipe." He tried the word out, quietly, to himself.

———————

(He knew the word *sideswipe*, and wondered.)

———————

The delivery boy rarely took part in the warehouse conversations. People rarely asked him anything, and he rarely knew what to say when they did.

———————

As the delivery boy went past the door marked SUPERVISOR, he looked down at his feet.

———————

And continued on to the far back.

———————

Uncle hastened through the door, bumped the delivery boy, grunted.

———————

(Asswipe.)

———————

The delivery boy had a piss in one of the two tiny bathrooms.

———————

Then he went through the door—the one with the number-lock on its knob—and skulked down another narrow and dark corridor to his area of the bunks. He looked around before stashing a few bills. Just a few. Wrapped in some bathroom paper, stuck to the underside of his soap bar, sealed in his soap box, zippered in his bathroom bag, placed in his shoebox, under his sandals, behind his small bag, under his bunk.

———————

Then he made his way to the storage rooms, and searched among the tall shelves.

The storage rooms smelled like aluminum and dust and wet cardboard and droppings.

———————

Uncle was not in his chair.

———————

The delivery boy saw a glue trap, half under a low shelving unit. There was something dark and matted stuck to it. The delivery boy kicked the trap farther under the shelf, and out of sight.

———————

Someone said something, and the delivery boy whipped around.

———————

It was only Wodge.

———————

The delivery boy waved hello to Wodge, who was balled up on the floor in one of the aisles, muttering to himself in that language only Wodge understood.

The delivery boy stepped over Wodge's weird legs, and delved farther into the long row of dark shelving, to claim his numbered delivery merchandise.

———————

He signed a clipboard again with the blunt pencil that was attached to the shelving unit by a fraying string. With his parcels in his arms, he maneuvered past a few warehouse men, went down another little corridor, to a small loading dock, where he squatted on his heels, pushed his back flush against the metal doorway, and watched the rain.

Five minutes, tops, he thought, taking out a brand-new cigarette.

———————

He drew deeply on it, unlit; tasted its baked, vegetal tang.

———————

On his way back out, he tossed Wodge an old butt from his cigarette packet.

———————

Wodge grabbed it up, put it in his mouth, and sucked on it.

———————

"Coming through."

———————

"See you," the delivery boy said, over his shoulder.
    "Uh," replied N.

———————

No rain again. At least.

———————

He peeled the bags off his body in ragged strips.
    Threw away the wads of plastic in a trash can.
    Back in the saddle.

(Molted.)

Little flashes on the street. Weaving around (the word would be *puddles*, but in this case, I imagine that the delivery boy would think of it as something more like *puh-duls*, as this was how the word was taught to him).

He thought of this teaching-talk of N.'s. How he was given one bit after another; only one sound at a time.

(When N. spoke to him in this way, and in this special tone of voice, the result was that the delivery boy felt as if N. had somehow pumped extra blood into him.)

A taxi pulled out on his right flank. He adjusted his grip.

Difficult intersection. He sped forward, too quick, and had to brake. He veered, tried again, let a car go ahead, another; a truck in front of him threw up rocks and dust. He shut his eyes hard, then opened them quickly, only to see a streak of yellow cross his lane. A bus loomed, and passed.

And then he was through.

Then: a straightaway.

When the power-assist was on, he could ride and relax.

Sometimes his mind would wander. He would look to the side, and be surprised by a driver's eyes, looking back at him. And he would look away quickly.

The street is no place to lock eyes.

Traffic. Crates had fallen from a truck bed. Smashed.
Honks.

Customer twenty-two: more food.

He picked the bag up at a quick-food place.

Some of the boys in the distribution center used to work
at places like these. In many cases, the establishments
were run by their own families.

Few such restaurants are still family-owned, so
many of these (waiters, busboys, hostesses, cooks—even
the managers who punched the overlarge calculators in
back rooms at night) have become delivery boys.

Everything falls (he thought).

———————

"Eventually," the delivery boy tried out, "everyone will be making deliveries."

He considered this idea, and considered his feelings around this idea, and found that he felt nothing in particular.

"Even Strongmen . . ." he continued, pushing the notion, but just then was forced to come to an abrupt halt, as a large, open moving vehicle was blocking access to the side street.

———————

Honks (more honks).

———————

1. Upside-down chairs. 2. A disassembled bed. 3. Lamp bases without shades. 4. A wooden box slatted with dinner plates. 5. Rolled carpets fastened with twine. Etc.

———————

Waiting in the line of stopped vehicles, the delivery boy looked around in all directions.

———————

Then made a short hop onto the sidewalk, drove ten feet, bounced back onto the street, and was moving again.

———————

An older woman.

"Sidewalks are for people," she shouted.

———————

The warehouse calls: a couple more packages to pick up from other pickup centers.

———————

He did these jobs only from time to time. It wasn't his job, but it *was* a slow day, and he should help out the other boys, and: How could he say no?

———————

This was how, on many occasions, items were stocked in the warehouse. And for some of the other delivery boys, this was their only job: to pick up packages from other shops, distributors, and warehouses, and transport these packages to the delivery boy's home warehouse for further distribution. These delivery boys did not make tips, and were paid in meals and bunks. This was how the delivery boy himself started out. Before N.

———————

(It is not difficult for me to imagine this life, this world. A kind of closed vasculature. Nothing outside of a system of deliveries that pass unopened from warehouse to warehouse.)

———————

(These were the saddest jobs, and it was a life that had almost become the delivery boy's own.)

———————

(Uncle, for instance, never even left the building.)

———————

(Once, after a delivery, while waiting for an elevator, the delivery boy had looked out of a high window, and saw a woman walking her dog on a rooftop, opposite. The woman and the dog wandered around on the hot tar until the dog finally lifted his leg. The delivery boy wondered then if the dog had ever, in its lifetime, felt the earth with the pads of its feet.)

(Like this.)

(So the delivery boy felt grateful.)

N.

What would he have done without her guidance?

He thought about the conductor of the youth orchestra, with the fancy yellow coat.

He considered the other delivery boy who (may have) moved upriver.

———————

He thought of Wodge.

———————

"why so slow2day" he thumbed into his device.
   Then:
   "rain u think?"
   Then he waited.
   (. .)
   Finally N. replied: "Come in."

CHAPTER NINETEEN

N. looked up from the screen to make a quick, subtle, half smile.

(Half smiles were N.'s only smiles—and even half smiles were, for her, a rarity. Her face was a marvel of giving away nothing. Of the upturned-mouth expressions, she preferred the smirk.)

(So this was an event of a sort. But . . .)

"Fuck off," she snarled at the delivery boy as soon as he smiled back at her.

He flinched. N. returned her eyes to the screen.

"Coming through."

———————

Back in the warehouse, he dropped off his items, then cross-referenced the numbers on his phone—the new pickups—with the numbers on the shelves.

V837 (small box).

H144 (three shopping bags).

———————

When the delivery boy had debarked from the vessel, they were collected into a large holding room. In the room was a very large crowd of people, and a large board, covered in numbers.

———————

Jammed up amid the others. He heard numbers shouted, mumbled, whispered, bawled. (Like this was a land that only spoke in numbers.)

———————

The French horn player from the youth orchestra was number 479.

The delivery boy had wanted to go with her, but could not.

————

(The delivery boy wondered what number N. had been given, in her holding room.)

————

Back in the corridor, he had to step over Wodge again, who was now on the ground in the tight passage (the ground was where Wodge always was).

————

Wodge looked up as the delivery boy walked by and blurted something unintelligible again. He was still sucking on the used cigarette filter.

"Hello Wodge," the delivery boy said in response.

Wodge winked at him awkwardly.

"Sure, Wodge, *sure.*"

————

Anticipating seeing N., the delivery boy increased his pace.

(Although he always did this going past the Supervisor's office.)

———

"You look pretty," he practiced, before pushing the swinging door in toward the dispatch corridor, knowing that he *would never.*

———

As the delivery boy came into the dispatch corridor, there was someone new at N.'s station.

A different dispatch girl.

His greeting to N. turned into a wordless exhale.

———

On a bathroom break, probably, he thought, entering the outside air.

Merde.

CHAPTER TWENTY

(Re *merde*.)

———————

(The delivery boy had been, in his homeland, a student of languages. He was not a total country bumpkin. Nor was he some kind of half-wit.)

———————

(I mean: neither was he some kind of *famous genius, brought low by circumstance*.)

———————

(But the delivery boy spoke languages other than his own. Just not this language, in this city, here. He will be knowledgeable in some ways, ignorant in others.)

———————

(Actually, his French was quite good.)

Scattered phrases came to him as he pedaled.

Une fourmi, de dix-huit mètres . . . the delivery boy remembered the children in his class chanting . . .

Ça n'existe pas . . .

CHAPTER TWENTY-ONE

"*Musician*," the concierge explained, holding the re-
ceiver up, while pointing to her ear with her other hand.
"Doesn't hear it ring."

———————

(Sometimes doormen or custodians or concierges would
call up to a customer, and the customer wouldn't answer
right away.)

———————

Sometimes a customer might not answer at all. Often,
after not answering, the delivery boy would have to move
on to his next delivery, but then, an hour or so later, this
same customer would call and complain, and N. or some
other dispatch girl would pick up the line and get yelled
at. Sometimes the Supervisor would get involved (the delivery boy never spoke to the Supervisor but N. would tell
him later), and then the delivery boy would have to be
rerouted back to the original delivery spot and his timing
for the rest of the day and night would be ruined.

———————

The delivery boy might wait to hear the customer's muffled "Hello?" on the line (as if the customer had *simply no idea why they were being called*) or a subtle change in the doorman's or concierge's expression, and by the time the doorman or concierge was replying "Delivery here," or "Your food," or simply "Package" (and once: "Your *errand* boy is here . . ."), the delivery boy would already be moving toward the elevator banks (knowing the rhythms, so on).

———————

This concierge was a young woman. You didn't see many of those, thought the delivery boy . . .

———————

The young concierge had called up two times already, and she had hung up twice, and was about to try a third time, when she cupped the phone, leaned over toward the delivery boy, and said, conspiratorially: "He's practicing. Just go up. I'll keep trying."

———————

The delivery boy pressed seven, but even by floor five he heard the music.

Growing as the elevator rose (as in a crescendo) and then, when the doors opened, it became abruptly loud. The delivery boy walked up to the doorbell and pushed.
    And waited.

The delivery boy was not confident that this doorbell actually worked.

The music went on.

The delivery boy tried again, and again.

No luck.

So he decided to wait for a gap in the notes before pressing the bell again.

He stood there, pointer finger poised over the bell, hoping for a silence, a rest between notes. He would push the button at that precise moment.

The delivery boy's mother had explained to him that they could not afford music lessons.

Some of the other children had begun to bring in strange, variably shaped cases to school. Long boxes, short ones, twisted tubes, geometric oddities, each made of dark cardboard, each with a handle. The delivery boy knew that each of these odd shapes must contain an instrument.

When he was a bit older, he would listen to the youth orchestra rehearse every week in the school's ratty auditorium.

He was, for these rehearsals, the only audience member.

———————

The orchestra was conducted by that teacher with the fancy yellow coat. The conductor was also art teacher, teacher of French, and coach of their sports team.

———————

One day, the orchestra was playing a particularly long and complex composition. The conductor was waving his arms about wildly, and just as everything grew to a fevered pitch, suddenly, there was a rest.

———————

The baton stopped in the air, bows stopped in the air, mouths froze, open to inhale the air, everything still.

———————

Eventually, the conductor dropped his baton arm, chuckled to himself. He scanned his youth orchestra. The children looked back at him. He shrugged, then he turned around to the (almost) empty auditorium.

He said something the delivery boy couldn't make out. Then the conductor put his hand up to the side of his mouth and shouted:

"Hey—"

"Uh . . ." (said the young delivery boy).

"Hey!"

"Me?"

"Yes, you."

"But I'm not—"

"Oh, for Christ's sake just get up here."

———

The conductor crouched down as the delivery boy approached the stage.

"I asked if you would play cymbals."

"I don't know how."

———

"You don't need to know how," said the conductor. "Just when."

———————

From then on, the delivery boy stood in the back of everything, counting.

———————

He never really heard the music anymore. Just counted. He didn't know if what they played was loud, soft, beautiful, ugly, major, minor, all he knew were bars; counting bars. And always, his brain would shout at him (especially during performances). It would shout, prematurely: *Now! Now! Now* . . .

———————

But he never missed his moment: splashing his palms together smartly.

———————

(Honestly, he never really *nailed it* either [and as the big clash approached, the conductor would always feel a slight nervous cramp begin to develop in his baton hand] but in the end the delivery boy was always just about close enough.)

The delivery boy began bringing his own instrument to school in a case. A perfectly circular case.

The Strongman came to one performance and everyone sang a special anthem to him before picking up their instruments.

They had been assigned a new conductor at that point.

Ding . . . dong!

CHAPTER TWENTY-TWO

Having handed over the small box, the delivery boy still had the three bags to deliver.

———————

Three bags was not the best. Even numbers were better than odd. Bags normally went on handlebars, so balance was an issue. But in this case, all three bags were light, so he was just fine.

———————

These three bags all looked the same, and told him nothing of their contents.

———————

The girl who played the French horn was, for the delivery boy, at first: "The girl who carried the big case that looked like a giant dark ear."

———————

As she walked by his stand from behind the stage, the delivery boy saw the black case, then the arm holding it. Then he saw her back, then the back of her head—her hair in plaits. She sat down directly in front of him, facing away, in the second-to-last row of orchestra musicians, behind which sat the delivery boy and the timpani player.

———————

He saw her: put her big dark ear down, unlock it, remove a bundle of red cloth, unswaddle the shiny brass horn, test a few of its valves, rest the horn back in her lap, pull a mouthpiece from the case, put this mouthpiece to her lips, give it two quick bursts of air, screw the mouthpiece to the horn, brush the horn with a few more quick little kisses, look up—brisk and alert—awaiting a downbeat.

———————

Naturally, the delivery boy had thought she was pretty. He had thought this even after (and maybe even especially after) the end of the rehearsal, when they were all packing up their instruments and accessories, and she slid the central U-shaped valve out from her horn, turned it over, and dumped all that spit onto the stage.

Puh-dul.

I am not a baby anymore (the delivery boy asserted to himself, suddenly alert to his own annoyance).

(No, the delivery boy was not a baby. He wasn't, strictly speaking, a "boy" either, though neither was he a man.)

(The delivery boy was an *in-between-er.*)

(He had a bit of a mustache, though it looked more like a smudge, partially erased. On his chin was also some sparse dark hair. But his cheeks still had that roundness that stubbornly refused to thin out, and the point being: from the outside—to those who didn't know him—it was very unclear what he was, exactly.)

———————

But N. had said, right at the start: "delivery boy."

So that was what he was.

———

("No names," N. also explained. No names—other than Uncle and Supervisor and Wodge, that is. Wodge was the only one with a *name* name, though the delivery boy doubted that this was even Wodge's actual name.)

———————

But the delivery boy had found out hers.

———————

He was proud of having found it out.

———————

(I imagine that, for him, it had been a proof of his dedication, intelligence, investigatory acumen, devotion. A demonstration of all these things. A bird at her doorstep.)

———————

One day, in her company, he spoke her name out loud, affecting a casual air.

———————

(Her real name. Not her number, not her first initial, nor the name of her job.)

———————

She held up a hand, stopping him short, and turned away without speaking. She refused to look at him for a while afterward.

———————

He worked hard to get back in with her, but she wasn't having it.

———————

(She was a "tough nut," even at the best of times.)

———————

(Red light, red light, red light, so on.)

CHAPTER TWENTY-THREE

She was less of a tough nut only after the incident.

———————

Which had been bound to happen.

———————

N. had seen the delivery boy stagger into the dispatch room, and she went to him, brought him to the back (practically carrying him), quickly past the door marked SUPERVISOR, whispering urgently to the warehouse men for help, wrapping him in her coat, and arms.

———————

"The bike . . ."
 She hushed him.

———————

(When a bike is broken, it is added to the delivery boy's debt-to-be-repaid.)

———————

(Many of them had accidents. Those who were debilitated—even for a short period—were moved on. Those who could manage deliveries still, no matter how painful, remained.)

———————

(The debt-to-be-repaid included the passage on the vessel, the phone, the helmet, the bungees, the bunk, etc.)

———————

N. visited him. She sat on the end of the crowded mattress. He was doubling up with another delivery boy then (*no deliveries, no bed*) and in these moments N. was the only girl in this boys' room. The delivery boy pulled the nubby, red blanket up to his chin. She spoke to him. She taught him new words and expressions.

———————

1. Tough nut. 2. Doorbell. 3. Secondary location. 4. Power-assist mechanism. 5. ETA. 6. Piling up. 7. Holiday . . .

––––––––––

(The debt-to-be-repaid is, of course, always being re-paid; never paid, which, of course, the delivery boy was smart enough to understand. He saw N. give money to Uncle, and understood that as well. He understood that the money was for Uncle's silence.)

––––––––––

Time passed in a fever. But eventually, he could straighten the leg and uncurl his back.

––––––––––

(And after this convalescence, he knew quite a bit more of the language.)

––––––––––

When he was finally able to leave the bunk room, he would wait for a time when Uncle was in the shelves, and the Supervisor was in his office or away, and then the delivery boy would come through to the front hallway and lie on the floor in the front, hidden under N.'s dispatch station. He would listen while she spoke to the customers and the other dispatchers, and clicked in the orders.

———————

The floor was made of dark rubber mats. It was not uncomfortable, but it was damp, and the mats smelled like street tar.

———————

(Was this how Wodge got this way—all crumpled up—I wonder? A delivery accident?)

———————

While the delivery boy lay on the mats, hiding, he listened to N. speak with the customers.

———————

He would also listen for the heavy tread of the Supervisor.

———————

If the Supervisor came out, the delivery boy would curl up quick, like a startled snake, so that his whole body twisted under the desk and was concealed.

———————

This would hurt like a fucker, to curl up like that.

———————

And there was real danger.

———————

(The girl covered her eye and turned away; the toothpick; the clank of the bar, set in place; the boy who had disappeared . . .)

———————

(Only boys who worked could stay.)

———————

(Except for Wodge, who was a mystery, and an exception.)

But the Supervisor never found out.

N. had spoken with the others as well. No one told. The delivery boy spent those painful days convalescing in secret.

When he tried to thank her afterward, she made an irritated gesture. (Flicking her wrist at the air, like a short backhanded slap.)

CHAPTER TWENTY-FOUR

The doorman held out his hand for the delivery boy's bags.

———————

"The customer's signature——" the delivery boy remonstrated.

———————

"If I let you up," said the man, as if merely pointing out a fact, "you'll dump your flyers on the doormats. You people leave your trash everywhere . . ."

"Yes sir, but——"

"Not if I can help it."

———————

No stars, no tip.

———————

One comment.

———————

———————

"You need to insist," N. pinged back to the delivery boy.

———————

"He said no."

———————

"Be a man about it." (She said.)

———————

("Be a man about it?")

CHAPTER TWENTY-FIVE

Be a man about it.

He kicked up the stand angrily and slid himself onto the seat.

Sulked.

Delivery *baby*.

The delivery baby missed all the lights coming back, and so squandered even more time.

A taxi-customer opened his door into a bike lane and if the delivery boy hadn't been paying attention . . .

———————

"Hey!" the taxi-customer screamed at him, in a surprisingly high, feminine voice. The driver looked on, blankly.

———————

N. was back again at her computer, but the delivery boy didn't look at her.

———————

("Be a man about it.")

———————

His pickup was up in the shelves. He had to use the ladder.

———————

D548, J549, B550 . . .

———————

Eight big bags. Uncle slumped there, watching the delivery boy struggle down the rungs.

Eight bags meant there would be four to a handlebar

———————

Wodge was still in the front corridor.

———————

Wodge spat out the butt he was chewing and grunted at the delivery boy, who stepped over him carefully.

———————

The swinging door. "Coming through."

———————

The delivery boy waddled out to the front. N. narrowed her eyes at him and said something to the other dispatch girl. They both looked at the delivery boy, arms folded across their chests.

———————

(With N. he always felt at fault. And his crimes were never given names.)

———————

Out at the rack, he struggled to get the last bag onto the handlebars. Two of the other delivery boys stood there, smoking. They also watched without helping.

———————

Pushing off on his bicycle was like pushing off a boat with too many passengers. The bike listed one way, then the other. But halfway down the block he stabilized, sat down on his seat, reached over and clicked the power-assist back on, and whizzed off.

———————

Customer twenty-five.

———————

"Put them down there."
    "Yes sir."

———————

"Call them *sir,* and *ma'am.*"

———————

"What if they are the same age as me," he asked N.

"Doesn't matter."

"What if—

"Call them *sir* and *ma'am.*"

———————

Exhaust. He pulled his shirt up and over his mouth.

———————

Often there is no other way to go than via the busiest of the broad avenues. This time of day, they are always like this. Jammed up. The number of vehicles intensified the heat. The rain had long since become steam, sweat, or just weight.

———————

Several more of these slow blocks. Of heat and noise, and the delivery boy: weaving precariously between the trucks, buses, cars, and trolleys. An ambulance trilled, piercingly.

After a block or two, the ambulance let out a longer, louder wail.

The conductor with the yellow coat had, once, drawn a shape on the blackboard of their music theory classroom. They couldn't see what he was drawing, only the back of his yellow coat. He drew an upper line first, then added a quick downward stroke, making, as he did so, a long *snnnnnniiikk*. Then he turned around:

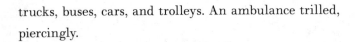

The siren moved everything in front of it forward, and suddenly he was out. Coasting again.

―――――――

During such moments, when he was out of the traffic, the delivery boy would click on the power-assist, take his feet off the pedals entirely, and slump in the saddle a bit. Take one hand off the handlebars and let it fall to his side.

Flip up the visor of his helmet.

―――――――

The bike drove itself.

―――――――

The delivery boy coasted along, all the lights turning green as if they were heralding his approach.

―――――――

(The delivery boy traveled the rapids of his unencumbered mind, and landed on Wodge.)

―――――――

He told himself: "The Story of Wodge."

CHAPTER TWENTY-SIX

Wodge was born into wretchedness.

———————

Wodge was born in a trash heap.

———————

(In a prison. A ghetto. A gulag. A landfill. A *burning ghat* ... Any of these will do, he thought.)

———————

Or, or, the delivery boy thought: Wodge was *not* born to wretchedness, but once lived normally, with a happy family—perhaps was rich, even. But then . . .

———————

(Gambling debt, addiction, market crash, plague, war . . .)

––––––––––

Wodge was the Supervisor's illegitimate son.

––––––––––

Wodge was the premature and malformed child of a poor dispatch girl, long deceased.

––––––––––

Or one of those girls the delivery boy had seen called into the Supervisor's office . . .

––––––––––

"STAY IN YOUR LANE," a woman gobbed out at him from a big green car's open passenger-side window.

––––––––––

For the second time that day, the delivery boy swerved violently, his bicycle wailing toward the curb, which his front tire hit.

––––––––––

The delivery boy bounced up once in his seat and came down again hard. Then everything toppled over.

The big green car continued on through the inter-section.

The delivery boy sat up, rubbed his knee and his lower back, and continued to follow the car with his eyes, stunned.

———————

Yes ma'am, he thought, with bitterness.

———————

His buttocks were also sore from the sudden stop.

———————

(He knelt, and rubbed them too.)

———————

What did *he* know of Wodge, after all, the delivery boy asked himself, as he rolled over and stood up.

———————

Less than nothing.

———————

He brushed off his knees and palms and thought:
So, by what right . . .

———————

He bent his neck toward his right shoulder, as if assessing the street . . .

———————

(. . . and "the whole situation").

———————

By what right. By what right, indeed.

———————

He picked up his bicycle. Once again, it seemed relatively undamaged. He checked the front rim, he checked
the power-assist. Pinched the tires. They were a little
low on air, but otherwise fine.

He got back on. Horns blatted around him. Someone's radio was playing.

———————

He pushed off and winced. And there was now gravel from the hot macadam in his right shoe.

———————

What would N. say if she had seen his daydreaming, he thought as he removed the shoe and shook it. She would call him a "stupid idiot of a boy."

———————

He set off again, warily.

———————

Anyway: he could "be a man," no problem. He was a tough fucker.

———————

That day, when the soldiers were bothering the orchestra girls, he had spoken up, hadn't he?

CHAPTER TWENTY-SEVEN

The rain, persistent, came back, though only for a moment.

———————

The street shone.

———————

And a broken fire hydrant gushed, redundantly.

———————

The rain shut off again.

———————

(The delivery boy found it difficult to square this need for *sir*s and *ma'am*s with the directive to "be a man.")

———————

His older brother had stood in the living room, waiting for him when he got home. His (younger) sister had looked away from the delivery boy, her forehead resting on the window that faced the dark street.

———————

(All the streetlamps in the city had been blacked out by then. Thus, the delivery boy had known that there was nothing for his sister to look at, and therefore she had been looking not at, but through, and away.)

———————

On that night, his brother had been uncharacteristically rough with him about the soldiers and what had happened.

———————

His brother told the delivery boy that he had acted like a fool.

———————

(Yes sir.)

———————

(His older brother had been rough with him because of his having got it all wrong, but the delivery boy could tell that his brother had been anxious as well as angry that night.)

———————

As if someone had been rough with his older brother as well.

———————

("Pull yourself together.")

———————

It must be a question—the delivery boy thought, later, as he stoop-sat, aggressively drawing on the remnant of a cigarette—of *when* one is servile and *when* one speaks up.

———————

His brother hadn't said this, but the delivery boy was now wondering about bravery, gallantry, and being a man.

———————

("You don't need to know how. Just when.")

———————

He stubbed out the smoke, licked his fingers and pinched it to be sure, and put the stub in his pocket (for Wodge).

———————

The seat of his pants was now wet from the stoop.

———————

As he was getting on the bike, someone yelled, "Hey, no smoking down there!" from an upstairs window (and the delivery boy wondered to what imagined effect).

———————

Upon coming back to the warehouse, the delivery boy stopped directly in front of the dispatch screens again. N.'s face was lit-up green.

———————

She looked up at him, and then back down again.

"What," she said.

"I have a thing for you," he said.

She continued clacking away.

"I have a *thing* for you," he said again.

The clacking in the room became a little quieter; the other girls watched from the corners of their eyes.

"Something. I have *something* for you. Not 'I have a *thing* for you.'"

"That doesn't matter," he said, diminished.

"Go away, idiot."

He did.

The delivery boy came into the small bathroom. It had the smell of having been recently occupied. He settled on the seat.

———————

(There was no gift for N., and he would have to figure one out.)

———————

Stupid, *stupid*.

———————

He pulled up his pants and cinched them high and tight. Pulled the chain.

———————

Warehouse shelves. Customer twenty-six: a small square box.

———————

"Fishing rod," cackled Uncle, looking at the box.

———————

(I had an uncle once who also made this same joke about any small wrapped present. *Fishing rod?* Or sometimes: *Tennis racket?* A stupid joke. An uncle joke.)

———————

In any case, the delivery window for this package was (unlike the package itself) unusually long.

———————

Extra time was good.

———————

Customer twenty-seven was up on Central Hill, at the Royal Arms apartments.

———————

(The Royal Arms was ten blocks from the Emporium.)

———————

There were bills in his soap dish, and bills in his mattress. There was a bill rolled up into the unraveled hem of his blanket. There was one bill in his one remaining book and some rolled in his socks.

———

No one saw.

———

"Remember about the *something*!" he exclaimed, not breaking stride, not looking back to see N.'s face, strutting awkwardly past her and out of the door.

———

The door jingled behind him.

———

(The delivery boy had not noticed the Supervisor behind the dispatch girls, working his toothpick.)

———

The delivery boy stood up in the saddle, put all of his weight into his left foot, and lunged. Once in motion, he clicked on the power-assist, and threw down the visor of his helmet with his palm like a snappy salute.

———————

Allez!

CHAPTER TWENTY-EIGHT

The Royal Arms apartment complex on Central Hill had ten elevators.

———————

(The elevator banks were opulent. Each door was framed with metal tracery, which made eaves and came to an ornate point, as if each car were a bower, or an altar.)

———————

A small crowd milled around the reception area, waiting for their numbers.

———————

The delivery boy was assigned elevator number nine, which went to the high floors.

———————

Though the elevators looked luxurious, they were actually quite old, and poorly maintained—cheap—and his car rattled as it ascended to the twentieth floor.

———————

The customer.

———————

(Routine tip. No stars, etc.)

———————

Back to the elevators.

———————

Delivery boys had been stuck in elevators before.

———————

It didn't happen often. But Uncle had told them all a story about a particular delivery boy who had disappeared and was presumed dead—robbed and murdered somewhere—but had turned up in a stuck elevator, dehydrated, but otherwise physically unharmed. That delivery boy had been in there for three days. (Uncle thought this was *hilarious*.)

———————

The delivery boy wondered if the boy who had been stuck had gone to the bathroom.

———————

The delivery boy (our delivery boy) had, himself, been in the toilets just earlier, but had not actually used them as they were meant to be used (as he was too worked up about the nonexistent present).

———————

Given (our delivery boy reasoned) that the (stuck) delivery boy would have assumed that someone was coming to rescue him any moment, the (stuck) delivery boy had most likely held off going to the bathroom. He would not have wanted to be discovered in an elevator filled with urine or shit.

———————

But there had to have been a particular moment when a line was crossed—when desperation got the better of this delivery boy, and he simply: let go.

(He must have felt ashamed.)

This line could have been crossed on the first day in the elevator (though this is unlikely) or perhaps sometime on the second.

What if it had been on the third? What if he had finally submitted to the inevitable only moments before he heard the clang, and saw the metal claw inserted into the doors . . . and maybe even watched from his helpless, squatting position, as the doors were pried apart . . .

(But this had been a different delivery boy. I only mention it now as *our* delivery boy's elevator—at the Royal Arms—also became stuck.)

Our delivery boy had been worrying a particularly difficult problem in his mind. Tenants got on and off the elevator car, but he was too busy with this problem to notice them. The elevator lurched.

———————

The elevator then lurched again, and made a grinding sound, and briefly, the lights had flickered. He looked up then, and saw that there were two other people in the elevator with him.

———————

There was an older woman, and a younger man who was about the same age as the delivery boy.

———————

They all looked at one another, shyly.

———————

They were stuck between the fifteenth and fourteenth floors.

———————

They stood in silence.

———————

After a period, there was a loud beep in the elevator and someone spoke to the tenants over the speaker. The young man pulled off his headphones.

———————

The delivery boy needed to piss.

———————

Eventually the older woman said something to the younger man. She and the younger man struck up a nervous conversation. They chatted, and laughed awkwardly.

———————

(No one knew what to do about the delivery boy.)

———————

Unable to piss, he went back to his problem, which concerned N., and how, though she helped the delivery boy, often at her own peril, she was also, quite often, very unkind to him. No matter how hard he tried, when he considered these facts the delivery boy could not manage to square them (though I find his confusion on this point surprising, I also remind myself that he was still young, and would imagine that a person must, perforce, feel only this way or that, rather than feeling several ways at once).

———

The elevator trembled, and all three people in it looked frightened.

———

(The delivery boy may have leaked a little, at this moment.)

———

He turned his mind back again to N.

———

(N.'s callousness, he thought—vaguely, feeling for the
contours of the idea—was like the timpanist's lapel
badge.)

———————

The elevator was still. The older woman and the
younger man resumed their uneasy patter.

The delivery boy went back to his problem.

———————

(The timpanist's badge was "the future," and this was a
point of pride for the timpanist. But he had been wrong.
The badge was not "the future"; or rather, the timpanist
had picked the wrong badge, and the wrong future. The
wrong future now being long past.)

———————

The elevator buzzed.

———————

Then it finally began to move again.

———————

Downward.

———————

(Albeit slowly.)

———————

The old woman audibly exhaled. Then she said something to the young man, who laughed, and said something back to her. They continued to ignore the delivery boy completely.

———————

The elevator made its laborious way down to the ground floor, and when the doors finally opened, the older woman and the young man took a step out, and exchanged a few words of relief.

———————

The delivery boy, who was still in the elevator, had to wait for them to stop talking in front of the doors before he could exit.

———————

A small crowd gathered around the couple. No one at the Royal Arms apartment complex noticed him.

———————————

(Which was an enormous relief.)

———————————

So he sped through the doors, and outside, over to the iron lamppost to which his power-assist bicycle was locked. He unlocked it. Looked at his device. Still plenty of time.

———————————

He felt in his pants pocket for the roll of bills. All good.

———————————

(The delivery boy was, then, at the very top of a hill— the highest point in the city. And if he had enjoyed even a little bit of self-possession in that moment he might have looked around him and seen the entire city laid out as a map, hatched with streets that sloped gently toward the bay, where the ferries and recreational boats began their journeys under the dark spans and up the middle of the bright river, which thrust out north toward Manor Grove and beyond. But he hadn't, and so didn't.)

On the bike and down the hill, and a short hop later and he was there—on the wide sidewalk in front of the Emporium, which was a market and a department store.

He squared his shoulders, and marched up to the long row of turnstiles.

He went straight to the toilets, unzipped, leaned his hand against the wood-paneled wall, and peed. This was also: *an enormous relief.*

CHAPTER TWENTY-NINE

The Emporium was a massive open space, divided into stalls.

————————

There was a gallery, from which customers ate and drank, and looked down on those shopping.

————————

It was too crowded.

————————

(Like a holding room.)

————————

(Never mind.)

————————

To get to his particular destination in the Emporium, he had to jostle his way.

———————

He sideswiped, frontswiped, and asswiped several of the other shoppers in the process, for which he apologized, though no one noticed or paid him any attention.

———————

He was in a hurry, yet he stopped three more times.

———————

He knew what he wanted, but needed to be sure.

———————

He visited:
1. The greenhouse, to look at the exotic palms and strange flowers available for sale.
2. The food stalls.
3. The perfumery.

———————

The accumulated aromas from these bazaars was far too intoxicating for him, and by the time he was sprayed by the young lady's atomizer he had begun to feel not a little bit dizzy. He sat down for a moment.

———————

And the music in the Emporium Market and Department Store was also loud, and surging.

———————

Things spun.

———————

He needed to go back to the toilets and wash his face in cold water, but did not have the time.

———————

He forced himself up, and pushed onward toward his objective, following signs that read JEWELRY CENTER.

———————

The Jewelry Center was its own mini-emporium, and consisted of about twenty individual stalls, each with glass cases displaying its particular specialty. Some stands sold watches, others rings. Some sold plates, candlesticks, centerpieces, commemorative coins. Everywhere the delivery boy looked there were precious metals and jewels.

———————

The place was wet with treasure.

———————

(It certainly did not occur to the delivery boy that much of this jewelry was paste. Not because he was poor, or foreign, or stupid—please—but because, again, he was young. And perhaps because no one can know *everything* about *everything*. Even at my age, now, I can't tell real from fake. I don't know why we should expect the delivery boy to have been able to make such difficult assessments. Anyway, some of the jewelry was valuable, certainly, but it was practically impossible to tell which pieces, among so much imitation. So.)

———————

The delivery boy found his stall. There was a long row of dark velvet torsos and necks.

———————

Against the dark velvet necks were a series of bright necklaces, set off, brilliant.

———————

He had ten minutes, tops, to choose, given the state of traffic and the time of day.

———————

Then he saw the large revolving-carousel display.

———————

Draped on its many arms were exquisite, delicate chains. Thousands of them. Each locked. Each ending in a delicate charm, made up of a name, spelled out in a flowing script.

———————

1. *Ada.* 2. *Adelaide.* 3. *Alma.* 4. *Agatha.* 5. *Arabella . . .*

He knelt down and spun the column until the *N*s were facing him.

He was on all fours. People walked by. He could see their leather shoes strike the floor near his hands. He hoped no one would tread on his hands.

There were so many names. So many . . . but then, there it was.

Should he?

("You needed to insist," N. had told him.)

(And: "Be a man about it.")

He called to a salesman, who looked him up and down.

***

The delivery boy got up from his crouch, wrested the roll of bills out of his pocket, and placed it on the shiny salver in front of the salesman on the glass counter.

***

The tightly wound bills rocked back and forth for a moment.

***

The man wrapped the necklace in paper, taped the paper up, and then put this parcel inside a small shopping bag.

***

The delivery boy had requested that the salesman staple up the shopping bag as well, which the man had done, reluctantly.

———————

The shopping bag went on the back rack, wrapped in the delivery boy's light jacket, and was secured with all four of his bungees.

———————

He was glad to be back in the air, in space, with only the sounds of the street.

———————

Once more, he turned his focus to the matter at hand, unlocking the bicycle, slinging the chain over his shoulder, standing bestride the frame and kicking off; thereby missing, again, the incredible—and quite famous—view from the top of Central Hill.

———————

On the trip back to the warehouse (if he hurried, he would only be a little late, so hopefully no one would notice), he thought only about the necklace.

———————

The necklace.

———————

(It had a kind of gravity that pulled all his thinking
to it.)

———————

The delivery boy didn't think once about the traffic or
his aching leg.

———————

He didn't try—as he sometimes did while he rode—to
sum up his tips for the day.

———————

(He didn't see anything around him, even neglecting to
notice the young women who, with the warm, clear
weather, had come out onto the broad plazas, boule-
vards, and side streets of the city, alone, in couples, gathered around in groups, looking at windows, clutching
schoolbooks, handbags, piloting scooters, guiding tour
groups, sitting at roundabout cafés, perched on the lips
of the city's gulping fountains, standing on balconies,

leaning over bars, lying on park lawns, their legs drawn up under them, or knees clenched demurely, tossing their hair, colorful silks tied loosely around their necks, cigarettes slanting down out of slender fingers, their reverberant laughter the tinkle of hundreds of shop doors opening, seducing the air, spirits and skirts rising with the heat and lifting the entire metropolis up and off like a zeppelin . . . The delivery boy paid no mind to any of this and could only think about the necklace—as if its gilded emblem had been burned into his thoughts like the afterimage of the sun.)

CHAPTER THIRTY

He mopped up his sweat with his thin jacket.

He pushed the front of his hair to one side using the flat of his palm.

―――――――

He entered through the front door of the warehouse.

―――――――

(Tinkle.)

―――――――

She had a phone cradled awkwardly between her ear and shoulder, and another phone in her hand. She was speaking . . .

―――――――

("*Mile-a-minute*. Means loud and fast.")

The delivery boy waited.

She eventually punched off her call, went back to the other phone, then ended that call as well.

She began clacking her keyboard.

He did not want to have to announce his own presence; so he waited.

He wanted *her* to see *him*.

And eventually, her eyes began to rise . . .

. . . then focus . . .

———————

She was startled by the poorly contained rapture on the delivery boy's face, and failed to adjust her own reaction accordingly.

———————

Briefly, for a moment only, she looked how she truly looked.

———————

The delivery boy saw her expression (and mistranslated it as a sign of sympathy toward him).

———————

(It had been sympathy: Pity, that is. Again, pity.)

———————

(Either way, the delivery boy should have known from past experience that he would have to pay for even this small revelation.)

"What the fuck are you doing?" she said, swiftly recomposing her features.

———————

He thought about the dances in the old public hall.

———————

Rules.

———————

"Well?!"

———————

The rules governing . . .

———————

"Go," she barked at him then, as if he were in the next room.

———————

"I told you before. I have . . . something for you," he re-plied, straightening.

———————

(A man about things.)

———————

He had forgotten to take the present out of the stapled shopping bag, and so, while she watched impatiently, he had to tear the bag open.

———————

(Not the flashy presentation he had envisaged.)

———————

He held up the small paper packet.

———————

"This is for you."

———————

(The delivery boy did not understand the new look on her face either. He thought she was angry.)

———————

"No."

———————

"Please—"
    She whispered loudly: *"Goaway."*

———————

She wouldn't look at him. She hammered a few keys on her computer, decided something, and stormed off from the station.

———————

He shoved his fingers under the folds of the parcel, roughly levered it open, and, pinching the delicate metal links, let the paper fall to the floor.

———————

Deaf to him, she hurried through the large, swinging door.

He followed, entering on its backswing, and he was in the narrow hallway.

He took hold of the ends of the necklace, insubstantial as thread, and held it up between his two hands.

He shouted.

"Hey," and she turned, and everything stopped.

(Another incredible silence.)

"Looks expensive," said the Supervisor, his languid, fucker's voice emerging from the darkness behind them.

PART II

When I make myself a sketch of N.'s face from memory, I can surely be said to mean, by my drawing: her.

CHAPTER THIRTY-ONE

"Where did you find my necklace," N. hissed, snatching it away from him. She glared, shoved the delivery boy in the chest, and turned him around violently. Then she gave him another, sustained push between his shoulder blades. He was forced completely out through the swinging door, face-first.

He found himself alone in the middle of the dispatch area. He turned back then, and saw, as the door rocked to a close (as I imagine it, now), a series of vignettes of diminishing length:

Swing: The Supervisor grabbing N.'s arm.

Swing: N. being led to the far door marked SUPERVISOR.

Swing: N. disappearing into the office.

Swing: The Supervisor looking directly back at him for a beat.

The final, slender aperture, which framed the Supervisor, going in after her.

———

The delivery boy heard, from farther back in the shelves, Uncle's low, hacking laugh, and from behind him, the tittering of the dispatch girls, then he heard a lock bar being clanked into place in the Supervisor's office.

The delivery boy walked away, and out.

He got back on his bike.

He tried to resupply his body with air, but his body firmly refused to accept any.

He kicked off.

He pedaled.

———————

In the warehouse corridor, Wodge had mumbled something. Wodge had been on the floor the entire time, sucking his discards and dog-ends. The delivery boy hadn't seen Wodge there either, hadn't seen anyone except N. Hadn't checked, or said his "Coming through . . ."

Looks expensive.

The delivery boy stopped at a dead end, sat on a bench, and waited, though he did not know for what.

He watched the tree across from him. He took out his phone. He watched a bare branch move in the wind. "I am sorry," he wrote, from the dead end, before pushing the back arrow hard, ten times.

———————

(*Dead end*, it means *no passage*.) No passage. To, or away.

More cars went by on the perpendicular street. He kicked the ground. He smoked. A kind of throbbing nothingness overtook him, before reformulating itself into anger. He swore at everything, including (especially) the unblemished and untroubled sky above him. He pushed his bike over with his foot, then got up and kicked it. He looked at the bike on the ground. He noticed a small light, emanating from under the handlebars, and saw that the flashlight he had taped there just that morning had been left on, and had burned down most of its battery charge. He flicked off the pocket light, then consciously, and with effort, sucked even more breath into his lungs. He let it out without any real relief. He picked the bicycle back up again. (He had only noticed the flashlight as the day, the ruthless day, was finally moving toward late afternoon, and he was, at that moment, in the shadow of the building behind him.)

"Where did you find my necklace," she had said, covering for him. Smart, he thought.

N.

N.

N.

(Etc.)

Then the phone buzzed and he scrambled to get it out from his pocket. He thumbed it to life.

Another delivery.

Simplest thing.

As if that was all there was.

(Even now.)

Pickup and delivery. Pickup and delivery.

Fast times, slow times.

"Come back now," she wrote.

There she was. Looking as she always did.

And she was standing out in front of the door to the building.

Then he saw four large shopping bags. All lined up in the front.

She had brought his deliveries . . . to him.

(Unusual, in the extreme. Though the delivery boy wasn't thinking of this. Of how unusual it was for her to have brought the bags out. And I don't blame him for not noticing, as he was too focused on N.'s face: trying to read its disposition.)

He stopped the bicycle in front of her and got off, letting it fall over. She ignored the bike, picked the bags up two at a time, and handed them over to him, not speaking, eyes downcast.

He took them, and put them down on the sidewalk next to the fallen bike. Three bags were heavy. The fourth was light.

———————

She spoke to him then, still looking down:

"A *very long* delivery."

(To a part of the city he'd never seen.)

"You do this, for him, now."

(Special trip. No choice.)

"Make it okay."

(Debt-to-be-repaid.)

"No fucking around."

(Of course.)

"Do *not* look in the bags."

(Bad omen.)

"I have to go back."

(But . . .)

"Go."

(Tough nut.)

He nodded, but paused before turning. He looked at her. And saw something in her expression that was brand-new.

CHAPTER THIRTY-TWO

He slid into the street, displacing humid air, and leaving behind him a thick fug of apprehension. He reached up to flip his helmet's visor down, but didn't. The air was warm, yes, but fresh, and he didn't want anything between him and it. The light: clear and yellow. He got off the bike, took off the helmet, and strapped it down to the rack.

He would: 1. Not fuck around. 2. Make it okay.

He straddled the seat, leaned forward and pushed with both legs, clicked on the power-assist, which ground out one single, concise complaint, before finding its groove and humming once more. He set off, up the wide boulevard.

A quick glance in the small round rearview and he saw the warehouse withdraw. The sidewalk outside it was empty.

Green light, green light, green light . . .

———————

He steered around (*slowpokes*), wove among the cars, finding lanes that shouldn't have existed, spaces that were folded and unfolded by the flow of traffic. He knew every move of each vehicle on the street and, anticipating, made the most of it, cutting up the roadway into unexpected shapes, his bike a blade, and he found himself laughing at drivers, taunting other delivery boys. He leaned far to one side and then corrected to the other, never having to stop at lights, at crosswalks, never having to dismount (dismounting at intersections: he thought of this as a failure in a kind of child's game, in which the pavement was made of fire). Soon the way opened up. Looking ahead as he coasted, he began to feel the neighborhood around him transform. But into what? All the streets and roundabouts he had become intimate with over those days and months (and who knows how long), those once-unknown streets that he had believed would always be part of a disorienting and alien future—this old route—was, perhaps, now, becoming precisely that: Old. Scenery. Part of the long unfurling of his past.

———————

He was moving toward something, and that something was: getting it right. This, he concluded, was being-a-man-about-things, which meant insisting, and then accepting (no, embracing) the penalties for such insistence; declaring one's feelings, and being rebuked if necessary (rebuked, sure, but no, not by her; not by her). This was it. And it turned out that timing had nothing to do with anything; nor counting; nor the *when* of it. It meant not waiting for a cue. But clapping those cymbals together loudly, at will. Early, late, whenever: but stopping everything in its traces. Yes, there were new debts-to-be-repaid, and yes, the new path was not without perils, but the delivery boy now noticed a fresh excitement surge out from some subterranean spring—an excitement at traveling outside the tightly belted limits of his old, circumscribed life. He was full up, ready, as if the world were suddenly and unaccountably available, affordable, proffered.

(The delivery boy, throughout these transports, neglected to consider N.'s expression as she stood outside the warehouse building: that look, an unprecedented, truly *unguarded look*, and what this expression might have truly meant. It was, in fact, the only sign he should have read more carefully. But he didn't. And again: How could he have?)

But then, in that moment, he felt nothing but this strange, upwelling sense of agency. He released his grip, tucked his legs up, closed his eyelids slightly against the almost tropical wind, and felt it play on his teeth and on the back of his throat.

He opened and closed his mouth.

And as he did so the wind in his mouth produced the *snap* of a bitten (red, yellow, green) fruit.

The bike ran, clicking, a bit hot, but fast.

The delivery boy saw the borderlands of his old neighborhood as a new series of discrete pictures, as if he were already transcribing the saga of his own great journey.

A tall striped stack made of stamped tin, jutting out of the middle of the avenue, gouting smoke. He and the rest of the traffic divided around it, and slackened, as if the street and all its noise, motion, and commerce (and even the delivery boy himself) were powered by currents of underground steam, which, now leaking, lost vital energy, and slowed the entire apparatus.

An old man, angled forward, bent almost in half as he walked, his hands clasped behind his back.

A young man leaning against a lamppost, smoking. He had a dog on a leash. A young woman approached, bent down, and spoke to the dog. The young man took a last drag of his cigarette, flicked it away.

The late-afternoon sun, perched directly on a chimney, like an egg in an eggcup.

A man flipping and dropping a coin, while another man watched.

A doorman spraying down the (already wet) sidewalk with a hose.

Three women gathered over a phone and smiling, as if they were bending over a cradle.

A man driving past him in a car that was shiny and yellow (and though the delivery boy thought the yellow was wicked, he wondered what it must be like to drive that car on days when the driver felt sad).

A (visibly) crazy woman, gibbering into a roadside helpbox.

A man carrying a mirror across a street. Which is to say: an unexpected (if brief, and blurred) portrait of a ragged, determined delivery boy.

———————

The wind against him, he chugged up a hill, and when he came over to the other side he saw the neighborhood's main commercial street, and the demarcation of its northern boundary. 1. Coffee chain. 2. Tobacconist. 3. Appliances. 4. Purveyors of Ladies' Underwear. 5. Sporting goods. 6. Bath balms and soaps. 7. Candy. 8. Computers, phones, and other electronic appliances. 9. Hotel.

10. Another coffee chain. 11. Fast food. 12. T-shirts. 13. Another fast food. 14. Shoes. 15. More clothing. 16. More clothing. 17. A retail park. 18. Pub. 19. Makeup store. 20. Mattresses. 21. Family restaurant. All fronted by glass display windows. People streaming in and out of oversize chrome doors, thumping music leaking out with the air-conditioning. Cars double-parked (always a hazard for delivery boys) and generally lawless sidewalks, swarming with tourists and shopping bags. People bustling, arguing, sulking. A child wailing. The atmosphere carried (like the atmospheres in municipal offices, or in waiting rooms) a mood of depleted power: the sense of a vital force having been sapped, despite the outward prosperity of it all. The delivery boy felt the energy leach from his legs, and for a brief moment it seemed as though he might have to get off his bike and rest (and he remembered how, in the Emporium Market and Department Store, he had sat down on one of the plush banquettes for only a moment; mirrors all around him, color everywhere, sounds bearing down, and the trouble he had had then, rising again, after having given in to the siren song of lethargy, which had overwhelmed him, the strong and suffocating lassitude) but not now—there would be no resting. Not with so much in the balance. He shook his head, slapped one of his cheeks, attempted to revive himself.

He pedaled. Several blocks later, at the next rise, he

saw, in a space between two large buildings, a view (a view from which he could see out farther). His head cleared instantly. The clouds ahead were massed into tall, pale towers against the yellowing sky. These clouds were north of the city, maybe over Manor Grove. Imagining the blurred outlines of his destination, out across the broad river, he then felt another, new kind of longing. He turned off the power-assist just so that he could feel his own muscles working. He needed the toil, after the shopping district, and he craved the horizon, and so he pedaled toward it.

("*Skim-ming*. It means he says you are stealing from him," N. had reported.)

Good, thought the delivery boy. Good. That *fucker.*

He biked faster, working himself hard, not noticing that he had just passed the boundaries of the old neighborhood and had entered a new one entirely.

CHAPTER THIRTY-THREE

That wind flattened his hair to the sides of his forehead, parting his mop directly down the middle. He peeked in his rearview, and chuckled. ("*Tu as l'air d'une noix de coco,*" the girl with the French horn had said to him, in French class. This, her opening gambit.) His hair always had this propensity to form a soft ridgeline along the crest of his head. (Then, later, after class, she had passed her hand gently across his uppermost hairs, teasing. "Quit it," he had protested, coloring happily.) He could feel her hand now, in the form of the wind, tickling at his roots. Even though he traveled directly in the breeze, there was something satisfying to him that it was blowing out of the north, as if this breeze were, like the clouds ahead—seen through gaps between the tall buildings—generated from the route's terminus. Out north. And just across the river. Like the air was coming to provide him with a foretaste of his destination. He dilated his nostrils and tried to suck it all in: those sun-warmed, gust-delivered molecules of Manor Grove (a job well done; newly achieved courage . . .).

As the delivery boy was working his way up and through the area lying between his old delivery zone and the outer quadrants of the city, his pants began to ride up uncomfortably, and his ears itched with perspiration. He stopped in the middle of the block and looked around.

Once thriving, he thought, assessing the area.

It was obvious, as apartments gave way to town houses—a dignified line of them, crenelated, mansard-roofed, behind high, wrought-iron palisades—and the avenues widened out, bisected by enclosed parks. The unlit streetlamps and unoccupied benches were curlicued, and he even noticed dull green, horse-headed iron hitching posts studding the way at intervals. But everything here was now abandoned, derelict, ruined. Many of the houses had windows missing, and the slate roofs were gapped and forlorn. A listing trellis, a scrawled warning or boast, patchy crabgrass, refuse piled up everywhere in corners. No pedestrians in sight. No other delivery boys. Cars had their windows up and didn't stop at the lights. This was, he decided, an impeccable backdrop for a haunting, or an assault. (He would know after all, as his own childhood neighborhood—so prosperous once, long before his time, with its fountains, broad avenues, and trim lines of poplars: a destination for local strollers and tourists alike—had, of course, after the insurgency, been reduced to just such an eerie state of abandonment and dereliction.)

He felt a tickle of fear, deep in his throat.

(Insurgency . . . Yes. Insurgency. But we could say: complot, junta, coup, putsch, popular uprising . . . Does it matter? Yes. But not here.)

And so he increased his pace, causing that same ridge of hair to tickle in the wind. He considered the helmet, but decided against it.

The girl with the French horn had lived, it turned out, not ten blocks from the delivery boy's own home. It was a spacious attic apartment. She had invited him—and a few other schoolmates from the orchestra—to a tea with her parents, a shy and nervous older couple, who laid out a lace-covered table with tea and sweets for them. After the parents withdrew, the delivery boy and the girl with the French horn had stood away from the others, looking out over the green rooftops, passing a hard toffee back and forth between them. The delivery boy had tried combing his cowlick down for the occasion, but it was not holding, so she licked her hand, candy-sticky, and flattened his hair. Just so.

Red light. Out on the corner, a woman and her bony little kid. She held him by one hand, and his feet only glanced the sidewalk. He cried, and the more he cried, the angrier she became, and the farther up and forward he was tugged by that meager arm. The delivery boy imagined the mother and a son not speaking the same language, and so caught up in a loop of miscomprehension. Like that. They crossed right in front of the delivery boy, not noticing him. The delivery boy checked the handles of the plastic bags, hanging from the handlebars. They were stretching a bit, but not too badly. The light changed. Months earlier, there had been a new arrival in the warehouse—another one of the many new delivery boys. (They came and went.) This one was also a bony kid. The delivery boy had recognized him from the holding room. In the holding room, Bony Kid had been called up to go with the girl with the French horn, when the numbers went up. They went to the same place, according to these numbers. Something had gone wrong though. After, somehow, the Bony Kid had made his way north (to this, our delivery boy's city) and when the Bony Kid got there, to the warehouse, he became another number: a delivery boy's number. The Bony Kid and the delivery boy (our delivery boy) didn't speak to each other more than was necessary. But one day when they were arriving at the racks at the same moment, the delivery boy asked the Bony Kid if he smoked, and they crouched in the doorway together and the Bony Kid took out a pouch and papers. They passed a rollup back and forth. (This thing—a passage on a vessel—was a shared history, but also a secret language between them, one they both understood, a language that included a cigarette, rolled in silence.) On that day, because the delivery boy had to know (or perhaps it was idleness, or perhaps some temporary and mistaken belief in his own resilience), the delivery boy asked the Bony Kid about what had happened to the girl with the French horn.

The Bony Kid did not know. Not really.

They had been sent out on different boats for the final leg.

Ah, said the delivery boy.

The Bony Kid had heard something though. He wasn't sure if it was true, but. But what; what had he heard? (Drag, linger, puff, flick.) The Bony Kid had heard that the girl with the French horn and the others with her were put out on a boat at night to cross a river, but the boat was, in fact, nothing more than a child's toy from a swimming pool, and that there had been too many people—the water was freezing, the current strong—and so after such a long passage, at the very last step of the way . . . The Bony Kid from the holding room trailed off, dropped and stepped on the ragged butt, and shrugged, beyond caring, really. The Bony Kid moved on from the warehouse after a few weeks, and that was that. (Moved on, or something else. It could have been anything. That "anything" could have been the Supervisor himself, who had never liked the Bony Kid—his fragility— which for some reason particularly angered the Supervisor, and the Supervisor might have simply "taken care of" the Bony Kid, to relieve himself of a nuisance—and what might have been an unwelcome reminder of the Supervisor's own, irrepressible urges. Though honestly, who knows. "Who knows," N. had said, conclusively.)

Never mind.

The delivery boy, drifting up the middle of the street, now approaching a traffic stop, also shrugged, also beyond caring.

"*Je suis une noix de coco*," he said, out loud to no one, adding, after a moment, "hard and sweet. Hard and sweet."

———————

The delivery boy obeyed the red lights. Mostly out of habit, as there was no one around to make him do so. He couldn't see a soul. As he waited for red, he heard a squeak, and craned. The delivery boy had stopped beside an empty schoolyard. The swings were moving in the wind. A small *puh-dul* had collected under each one, as if children had melted there. He shuddered, and then pulled out, for the first time ever, before the light changed.

More dilapidated town houses then, their front yards high with weeds. There was a stray dog, sitting in the middle of the road. The delivery boy slowed, and thought that he would love to touch it, say hello. The feel of its yellowing fur . . . but. 1. "No fucking around." And 2. The dog might be mean, and a biter. So the delivery boy carefully steered around it. The dog didn't budge, not even a little. Didn't so much as look his way. Just continued sitting there on its haunches, staring out at whatever it was it was interested in (food) or afraid of (another dog perhaps). The delivery boy was getting that feeling again—that "garbage ghost" feeling, and he wondered then if he were even there at all, present—discernible and distinct from the hydrants and manholes and awnings and smokestacks and trash and trucks and lampposts and so on. He looked back at the dog he had just passed, and let out a howl, his voice coming out surprisingly rough, and embarrassingly loud.

The dog simply continued his vigil, untroubled.

Then there was a long stretch of empty street again.

("*Neigh-bor-hood* means *area*," N. explained, as they bent over his device and its map, early on. The city was patches of simple, bright color. He had been reminded then, for the first time, of the picture he'd seen, of the town and the river: *the entire world in miniature.* But here, "the entire world" was an entirely different one. Central Hill, Town Hall, Downtown, Riverfront, Parkview, Suncrest, High Street . . . Then, farther north, what he learned were "bad neighborhoods." These lay between Downtown and the river. "*Bad neighborhoods* are where delivery boys get robbed.")

She never sent him there. (The warehouse rarely sent anyone to bad neighborhoods—not out of fear for the well-being of the delivery boys, but because the Supervisor did not want to risk losing his property to thieves.)

There had been robberies anyway, in the other neighborhoods. Of course. Robbery was a big part of delivery life.

But the delivery boy had been spared

———

1. Red. 2. Green. 3. Green. 4. Green. 5. Green. 6. Red.

(The delivery boy observed, but now disobeyed all of

these prompts. He did not think it interesting, how, under this new dispensation, the colors might revert to being once again: colors. Though I find it interesting, now.)

Red light (whatever) and then: another stretch of nothing. No people, dogs, cars. Farther down the same road, he stopped to reattach the flashlight, which had begun to become loose on the handlebars, and rattle. Then a set of area boys leaked from a hole in a fence, loitered for a moment to tie shoes, lean up against one another, kick trash, write on the letter box with fat markers, exchange a few jabs . . . Then they spied the delivery boy and began jeering at him. The delivery boy was sufficiently far away to feel emboldened, and made a rude gesture in their direction.

The area boys, far off, conferred with one another briefly, and then, suddenly, exploded, like a flock into flight, sprinting toward the delivery boy.

Oh . . . *fuck!*

The delivery boy spun the pedals into position and tapped on the power-assist.

Except that it didn't turn on.

He tried again.

(A few facts the delivery boy bore in mind throughout the assault: Delivery boys are and always have been obvious targets for robbers. 1. Delivery boys are vulnerable, not knowing the people, not speaking the language, not knowing the culture, not participating in city life as valid citizens, etc. 2. They are unarmed. A Supervisor would never allow an armed delivery boy, as such a delivery boy could turn on a Supervisor. 3. They carry valuable items, i.e., the items they are charged with delivering. 4. They carry money, meaning: the money their customers pay them for purchases and deliveries, and the money the customers tip them.)

The delivery boy had heard stories of all kinds of robberies: including one in which a delivery boy was robbed merely for the bag of food he carried. The robber ignored all the tips the delivery boy had been carrying on his person—his pockets quite literally bulging with bills—yet the robber had only demanded the delivery boy's containers of rice, and his meat and vegetables. He had heard stories of delivery boys who had been robbed with 1. Guns. 2. Knives. 3. Swords. 4. Spears (!). 5. Hammers. 6. Clubs, bats, sticks. 7. A chain. 8. Fists. 9. Feet. There was once a delivery boy at the warehouse who had been kicked so badly (in both ears) that the dispatch girls had to yell when they addressed him. He was not unique. Several of the other delivery boys in his warehouse had been messed up badly. One had been robbed for his shoes (a pair of red-and-yellow sneakers the delivery boy had been particularly jealous of). So it was quite reasonable to assume that many of the delivery boys who simply disappeared from the warehouse had perhaps met bad ends at the hands of thieves; and this possibility had been teasing at the edges of the delivery boy's mind, despite N.'s stories (*who knows*) of new lives in better places (the delivery boy had become troubled by a particular worry: that the bodies of at least some of these "moved-on" delivery boys would one day float ashore, or be dug up by a dog, or found in a refuse bin, and he had even suffered a dream once, that all of these "moved-on" delivery boys—those who had left or were missing—had been laid out in the middle of the street, all along the delivery boy's own route, in regular intervals, like railway ties. The delivery boy's dream-bicycle had taken the bodies like speed bumps, as he cringed above his bouncing seat. It had only been a dream of course. Still, he wasn't stupid. (As I've already asserted—except, that is, when it came to N., and *that* stupidity wasn't stupidity either, really, but rather a lack of conviction. But he never mentioned his worries and suspicions concerning the missing delivery boys to N., and I suppose, now, that he *was* uncharacteristically savvy enough on this front to know that her stories, the ones she told him—the reassuring ones, that is—weren't truly meant for him at all.)

But since the incident in the hallway, all neighborhoods were newly open to the delivery boy, and with the widening of his compass, so the potential for risk, meaning that this gang of area boys—the ones who raced toward the delivery boy (rage—mixed with some kind of atavistic joy at the hunt itself—overwhelming their features as they came on) did not come as a surprise, exactly, to the delivery boy, but more as confirmation of the fact of dreams as omens, and he pedaled hard in this semi–dream state (which was most likely—I am thinking—a species of shock), his power-assist mechanism sputtering and whining. The area boys huffed forward (they were unaccountably fast, as a mob in a dream about dead delivery boys might be), and the delivery boy drove faster and faster then, the boys screaming obscenities and running at him full-bore— the *fuckers*—and he punched the mechanism again, but: nothing. He punched it once more (*Again, with feeling*), hard, with the inside of his fist, displacing the plastic water bottle he had wedged in between the frame and the motor. He heard the bottle fall with a dull crunch behind him, and more frenzied shouts. He didn't want to look back, but did, and they were gaining, howling with that nonspecific hunger while he punched the power-assist again, then again. The voices were so loud

192

now, and close. Only barely behind him. It would be a matter of seconds. Closer and closer. It was as if they already had him. Had got him, before the chase even. Then a hand touched his rear fender . . . and the gears finally engaged, the bike jumped a little, and suddenly accelerated.

Shoved all the way backward by the sudden speed, mechanism burning hot between his legs, his thin jacket ballooned and luffing behind him, wind whipping at the delivery boy's face, he adjusted his posture, leaned forward then, prayed, and a few minutes later—a few minutes during which everything lay in the balance—he was sufficiently brave to check the rearview again. He saw:

A small cloud of dust.

The area boys, far back, slowing. Jerkily.

Them, stopping, no longer shouting.

Them—small now—bending over . . . panting.

Them, tiny, then.

Them, gone.

Again, with feeling . . .

They had tried, to no avail.

"Look here," the conductor said, lowering his arms and shaking out the sleeves of his yellow coat, "this, what you are doing now, it sounds terrible."

In such instances as this, when the orchestra's playing failed to speak, the conductor made them narrate the piece in question; made them translate the music into words. They'd take turns. (The delivery boy never raised his hand to volunteer.)

The concertmaster and first violin, a stocky, confident boy, two years the delivery boy's senior, the son of a local lumber worker (and one of those children who wore a small badge on his lapel), told a brief but surprisingly fervent (if overwrought) story concerning a boy (clearly himself, thinly disguised) who, amid a coalition of like-minded heroes, rises up against (a vague, generalized) oppression. The story (hammy though it was) fit neatly to the swells and dips of the work the youth orchestra was rehearsing that day (re dips and swells) and the story he told was provocative, and visibly angering to some of them (the trumpet player in particular, who muttered rancorously under his breath, which caused the woodwinds to snigger), yet the conductor was clearly pleased with the boy, the concertmaster (who, also, re dips and swells, had died quite early on in the conflict— not in the made-up story he told the orchestra), and after the conductor calmed the tumult with a few clanging raps of his baton on the music stand, all the children (regardless of their position on the divisive tale) picked up their instruments (what a wonderful sound—as I recall it now—the unintentional music of the-pickings-up-of-many-instruments) and played the piece (*Again, with feeling*) and it was as if the piece had been reanimated, infused with a remarkable new life, as music is a language—one that tells stories—and the orchestra occasionally needed reminding of this. The new music (the programmatic music of the boy's story) was animated by import, like a flat note imbued with vibrato (a technique denied the cymbal player, who had only two settings: *on* and *off*) such that it was as if the music were a different music, the instruments, different instruments, and even they, themselves, different children.

(It had been a lesson—had the delivery boy been keen enough to glean it—about the relations between meaning and feeling. And perhaps also a lesson concerning the relation between feeling and folly. But then, I am old, and tend to see lessons everywhere.)

In any case, at the end of the piece, after the sounds from the coda drifted away, the conductor let the silence hold awhile. Then he put his baton down on the lip of the music stand and said:

"Well now."

"Well now," the delivery boy said to his power-assist, having escaped a beating and almost certainly a robbery as well, and he laughed to himself, trying out a little bravado. His new story: the-overcoming-of-difficulties. The new character: the-boy-who-laughs-at-danger.

His chest swelled.

(Then collapsed.)

Poule mouillée.

Stupid, he thought, later, at an even safer remove.

(Delivery baby.)

He took a series of random turns then—making a new, meandering route such that he couldn't be followed by that gang of area boys. He knew he was now moving roughly north, but he still had to get back on track (*No fucking around*) so he stopped, and recalibrated, and several turns later, resumed his original course. He watched the device, now strapped to the handlebars next to his flashlight, to ensure the map had been updated. It had been. The red dot that represented the delivery boy was set three-quarters of the way through the bad neighborhoods. Pretty far in. And not too far—not too far for him to go—until the river now.

The river, a wavering green line on the map—a mere fingernail away (in map terms).

He was getting there.

He looked at the street beneath his tires, and imagined himself setting down new furrows over thin traces of the old. (Not fucking around; making it okay.) Still, the late afternoon began exacting a price—his clothes wet with perspiration after his huge exertion earlier — and he realized that he was very thirsty.

He was pedaling again, resting his power-assist for those farther legs of the delivery and for the trip back, when it might once more (he calculated) become crucial to rest, and as he stood above the saddle, his torso bobbing, his throat drying, his skin taut, his calves and thighs beginning to ache, he knew that he would need water soon.

Then the road he was traveling on met another, which veered in from the side; and both these roads met yet another, perpendicular road—the three roads forming a small triangular park. Triangular parks had been common in his homeland (as in mine. For instance: that large common that I have forgotten the name of—though I can picture it as clearly as if it were in front of me now—the one with the colorful marionette theater, and the streaked green copper statue of the man upon the rearing horse; the statue that was later toppled; the park with the hedging and parterre that was later mulched so that the space could become a military parade ground and garrison) though triangular parks were rare in this city, and so it instantly evinced in the delivery boy a feeling of familiarity, and nostalgia. The closer he came though, the less this triangular park looked like any of those from his native city. There was no grass on the lawns, there were no people on the benches, and the gazebo was cheap and empty. He scanned the park for a water fountain but did not see one. Only an empty, broken birdbath. Then he saw the telltale bright yellow of a corrugated sign, facing him at one corner of the triangle. A grocery.

Water.

So he pushed onward, coasted the last few feet, got off, and locked the bike to a small and denuded tree outside the half-gated entrance.

He approached the door and ducked his head under the iron grille. The door was shut, but he could see a bit through the dirty glass. The grocery was empty, as were most of the shelves. None of the overhead lights were on. He listened . . . nothing. A glassed-in cooler case stood against one wall, lit up faintly, hardly stocked. He saw 1. A few bottles of beer. 2. A jug of what must be long-expired milk. 3. A few liquor bottles. 4. One or two cans and bottles of soft drinks. 5. Dust. There were lottery tickets on the floor, and a mop leaned up against a shelf. He put his hand up to wipe the dingy door, and peered through the rough circle he had cleaned over to the counter and the register. No one there either. He saw that the register drawer was open. He looked behind him to the street, and the park. No one. He turned again, and put his hand on the door, testing, felt it yield, but just as he was about to push his way on through, he remembered about bells, and, instead, eased the door open slowly, and quietly.

"Hello?" he said.

No response.

He walked over to the cooler, looking this way and that, and, satisfied he was still alone, opened it. Cold, stale air. He stuck his head in farther. Ah. He leaned in until his chest was in the cooler as well. He could feel the sweat on his face and neck evaporating, and he shivered. His forehead was now touching the bumpy glass of a beer bottle. He opened his eyes and saw that there were a few dead insects on the bottom of the cooler. He stood up again, scanned the cooler one more time, reached out, and grabbed a red-flavored pop. And when he turned around again, there was a man behind the counter. The delivery boy heard the register drawer ring closed.

"Can I help you?" asked the man.

"Sorry."

"For what?"

"The drink—"

"Shouldn't be too pricey, let's see . . ."

(*Looks expensive . . .*)

The grocery man bent down behind the counter, before popping back up again, now holding a binder. He licked one finger and began to leaf through.

The delivery boy, having taken this opportunity to quickly rummage through his own pockets, found nothing there.

Wait, his shirt.

(Having found the appropriate page in his inventory, the grocery man ran that finger of his along the page in steady rows . . .)

In the delivery boy's shirt pocket was something. He pulled out a single bill. Not much, but.

The man's finger stopped moving, having found what it was looking for.

"See, here we are," he said, finding the price for the drink, and matter-of-factly naming it.

"*How much?*" the delivery boy asked.

The grocer repeated the price.

There would be no change.

The delivery boy would have nothing left.

(But what would the delivery boy possibly need more money for on that day, of all days?)

Back out on the street, the delivery boy cracked the dusty bottle cap and twisted it off, listened for a *fizz* he very much hoped to hear, and, satisfied, took a deep breath, swinging the red liquid up and into his mouth. It flushed down his throat. A continuous stream. The almost unbearably sweet and sunny tang of cherries suffused his nostrils (I once received a dark, shining cluster of cherries from my parents as a gift; they had been rare, then) and he drank until there was nothing left but the sound of a hollow slurp. Behind him, he heard the shop's grate close the rest of the way, and the sound of a lock being snapped shut. He was alone once more.

He walked across the street and over to the rotten gazebo where he had seen a concrete bench. He picked his way cautiously around the trash.

He sat. It felt damp.

The dampness did not come from the bench, but from his clothes, damp with sweat and the earlier rain. After today he would need to wash everything. Though he owned 1. Two T-shirts. 2. One regular shirt from home, which he never wore. 3. Two pair of socks. 4. One sweater. 5. A wool hat. 6. And his jacket. All of which he kept, when he wasn't working, balled up under his bunk. He only had a single pair of pants, which he now had on. These would be close to worn through by the end of tonight, the delivery boy thought. Where would he get more? At least he would clean everything. He didn't want N. to see him this way. (The delivery boy washed his clothes by hand in one of the warehouse bathrooms, using the hand soap. He did so at night, when everyone was asleep so that he could use the sink without someone banging on the door.)

He raised up off the bench and looked down and back. The seat of his trousers was thinned and shiny. Washing them would be fine, but some more permanent solution would have to be found eventually. Then he considered that—now that he and N. were closer, and shared secrets (a real transgression even, plus that *new expression* of hers—albeit, improperly understood), he could ask her advice on this particular matter of finding new clothes. Things would most certainly be improved in every way when he returned from this mission of his, and a new outfit—if it could be found—would be just the thing to signify such (positive) changes.

Preparing to relish this state of affairs, the delivery boy pulled out his yellow lighter and shook it; gave it a solitary scrape.

———————

Then he heard a grunt, and spun around, and saw something: a horror, a man or monster, its hair matted into thick and dusty ropes—its swollen, broken face without recognizable features, thickly encrusted with something dark, as well as an impasto of some yellowish gum, like rubber cement, or something stranger and far worse. Beneath the layers of soot and muck, the delivery boy could make out a chaotic outfit, made of disparate parts: newspaper, tinfoil, toilet paper, magazine pages, part of an old plastic washbasin dangling from where a neck might be, two enormous unlaced boots, one veering off at a strange angle from its twin. There was an overwhelming smell of corruption, decay, and waste (the vessel, the vessel), and the delivery boy jumped up to his feet and was ready to run before even being conscious of what confronted him there, and by the time he anticipated it stepping toward him, the delivery boy was already scrabbling away.

My lighter, he thought later, back on the bike, his new, brave manner thinned out (along with the seat of his trousers). He was pedaling (a mile-a-minute). His mind, meanwhile, held a single image: in the park, of himself, throwing his arms up in alarm and leaping over the gazebo bench. The lighter would be somewhere in the sodden mud. Just another lost article in a long list of lost articles.

(Tant pis, poule mouillée.)

He attempted one more heroic laugh. A laugh at the

absurdity and at fate, a laugh at the abyss, a laugh that could only ever only come out as the word *ha*.

(Impostor.)

Keep moving.

(Phony.)

Not a person after all, but a pile of rubbish.

(Fake.)

His ankle hurt, and he looked down and saw that the bottom of his pant leg was torn.

His phone buzzed, and he braked.

—On time?

———

—Yes. (He replied to N., wanting to say more.)

While he was stopped, he examined his torn trousers. He saw then that there was a thin gouge on his calf, not huge, but it stung. He dabbed at it with his finger and grimaced. He must have cut it on the bench, when he sprang away and out of the gazebo. A poor way to get wounded, he thought. A coward's wound. But there was nothing to be done about this, and he would ignore it for now.

Back on the seat, he surged onward.

On and on.

There were a few people out on the street once more. And the scenery had begun to improve a bit. He looked up and saw that there were a few of those yellow-flowering trees in full blossom, draped over the avenue. (The best week here.) The sun still raked at him, but under the trees at least, it was darkening and cool. As the bike cruised along, he heard a loud *ding!* (an unmistakable sound for those like me who came of age in a city of trams) and turned to look over his shoulder, and saw a red trolleybus coming up behind him. The delivery boy looked down at the road and saw two inset iron rails, worn to a vivid shine, lying on either side of his own bike's front wheel. He edged over one rail to the side of the road, and the driver—person in a green jumpsuit and cap; the only person in the otherwise vacant car it seemed—rang the bright yellow bell once more, perhaps as a greeting, or in admonition, or maybe as a goodbye. It rumbled past, after which a small disembodied hand—a child's hand—popped up in the trolleybus's rear window, and waved, slowly, to the delivery boy, before withdrawing, back below.

Buzz.

—Bags okay?

He stopped again.

—Yes. (He replied once more, not irritated exactly, but disquieted.)

———

Looking over, he saw that the bags were, indeed, okay (there was nothing truly okay about them in the deeper sense). He turned right, and shot down a narrow lane. Then left, on another. This led to a wider (yet empty) boulevard, which he entered with a little spurt of speed. His hands shifted, his weight redistributed (or something like this: and, I could no more narrate all his precise movements, subtle adjustments, flashes of navigational inspiration than he could; in fact, had he even been made aware of such crucial, minute, unconsciously coordinated decisions, even for the briefest instant, he would have fallen right over on his bicycle, or else driven into a tree. All his foremost thoughts were feelings.). Though the delivery boy did, gradually, become aware of how empty this section of city was.

No one, again. Not a soul.

The delivery boy had been thinking about the bags, of course. And he had some guesses regarding their contents, none of them cheering.

He knew it would be bad in there. How bad? Impossible to say (he heard the bar locking into place—imagined a red-clouded eye in its darkening yellow socket . . .).

It would be bad, what was in the bags.

Bad. But he was not going to look. So.

It was so quiet in this strange neighborhood. The only sounds—music, voices—were muffled, as if life itself were far off; or underground.

Houses here were scaled with vinyl. A few blocks on, the houses became cheap, redbrick. After a while, these brick houses clustered, clumped into larger apartment blocks. Huge, dull. Windows blurry as cataracts. Balconies strung with laundry. The storefronts grated or boarded up. Shoes hung from wires.

Not a single person out on the dreary forecourts. Thick glass doors: Scratched and written on. Everything written on. Road, walls, lampposts, park benches, cars . . .

This was a truly poor place. It seemed to him then like the city had fallen to pieces here, as if the area were a pile of scree in a ravine, fallen from the true city above, or rather, that the city had dispersed itself, and all of its energy, into a kind of dead and poisoned runoff. He thought of the hill with its stream of rainwater, and the grate, with its garbage, and his lock and chain lay heavy, wrapped across his chest like an ammunition strap. Out here, in the metropolis's festering spillage, he would have to be brave; a soldier. A soldier. Not a boy, not a man, but a soldier. (Some of the regiments back home wore their bandoliers crossed, in large Xs across their chests. Others had different signs: armbands, or small lapel badges, for instance.) The delivery-soldier looked about him, assessing danger, points of attack and vulnerability. His legs toiled. The landscape moved, cumbrously. Storefronts became empty lots. Then large blocks of storefronts and housing units became factories. Fences became chain-linked. Carparks, depots, municipal storage facilities. A few scattered, shapeless men drifted between walls, across lots. He was, he realized, leaving any vestige of the residential neighborhoods behind him now. Even those poor residential areas were giving way to something else. There was a large train yard on his left, and a large, conical mound of gravel, like the bottom half of a spent hourglass. The uncoupled train cars in orderly rows like shoes by the door. Immobile, darkened, going nowhere, perhaps ever again.

Loose sheet metal thundered in the wind, and so did the razor wire that topped the many chain-link fences. A tension filled the empty spaces. A small group of skinny women at the corner. Later, a man, next to a long-since burned-out vehicle, holding a bat. The man watched the delivery boy fly by him with murderous intent. Shopping carts, metal fragments, shining in the mud, an old chimney in an empty space. A tower with no windows. His throat was tight. He felt (it wasn't even sadness, but) a sonorous vacuum. Things were so grim out there that—when the delivery boy tried to imagine his future, when this journey of his will have ended—he knew he would not even be able to brag about this bit. He almost wished then that he were back in his bunk, wrapped in his thin blanket, amid the heat, smells, and snores of the other boys. But he did not wish it completely. Wishing one was elsewhere (he knew from experience) was dangerous. (This wishing always leads to other elsewheres, better elsewheres, to be wished for—one after another—the best of these elsewheres being elsewheres to which there is no possible return.)

He increased his pace, standing up once more on the pedals. Bore down.

Green light, green light, green light, then: *no light, no light, no light . . .*

He was heading out.

It was obvious.

The city was retreating, as if in preparation. Perhaps he would not so much leave the city as the city would simply evaporate around him. The warehouses were appearing farther apart, the neighborhood thinning, and suddenly the avenue had become larger, other roads merging in from both sides. After being the only moving vehicle for so long, he was suddenly startled to find that there were cars and big trucks all around. It was like an ambush. That is: before he knew it, he was completely hemmed in. And everything was moving faster. He was in a sluice, all these vehicles running on a torrent. No stopping any of it. He held his lane as long as he could, but once, twice, had to weave, and swing into gaps, here and there, as he was hard to see, was greatly at risk, small, on that accelerating, swelling speedway.

He clicked on the power-assist, praying. It ground its gears and then locked in, as he felt a heat rise up next to his inner thighs. Please, he thought, and gears continued to find other gears, though the power-assist made an unhappy sound, which he could make out even under the swooshings and pulverizing downshiftings of the larger trucks. But it was working. At least this.

There was no avoiding the fact that—on a road like this one, swollen with traffic—he'd need the power-assist, impaired as it was. More vehicles gathered, came out from the side streets, surfaced from tunnels, merged in from overpasses. They were heading away now, all of them. And as the buildings ended completely, and the sky loomed large, more and more tributaries joined, and the converged roads formed what could only be called a highway (the delivery boy's first experience of one) and the delivery boy edged his way, still at great speed, over to the far side of the road, as far as he could go in that direction, his bicycle bumping up and down violently, on the poorly welded joints between the blocks of the freeway, on the gravel and trash, a flattened milk carton, a bottle cap (and, more ominously, a ruined delivery envelope), jolting up on the large, parenthetical metal plates and grilles that patched the pavement, hazardous for bikes, the delivery boy hoping for his tires not to lose their grip, slide, or catch on one of them, praying for a smaller, more out-of-the-way lane, a cordoned-off space where he wouldn't be swallowed whole by one of the clanging metal giants that continued to amalgamate into the rush, dwarfing him—unarmored, on his puny bike, the stage much too large for his pitiable conveyance—and as everything continued to quicken, he suddenly dodged a large, rusty muffler that one of the trucks had long ago sloughed off onto the roadside like a prehistoric shoulder bone, and as he wobbled and jostled, he saw what he hoped was the ragged beginnings of a line, a new line on the road, a line that demarcated a path for him (a bicycle lane!). And having seen it, he veered, suddenly, between two pylons, honks complaining behind him at unaccountable volumes (the sounds of deep, downward glissandos, dopplering away), until he was successfully delivered onto this new track, and then, then, he could squeeze his handlebars, beginning to brake, just a little, to slow the bicycle (and life itself), to begin to relax, to breathe, to look around him, as tremoring aftershocks rippled through his body, and the chain link fell away, and the railings fell away, and he realized that he was on a ramp—no, a runway— and the sky opened up farther, and farther, deepening even as it came nearer, and then the road rose into it, up and up: and then he was out on the bridge.

(When I was a boy, I lived on a hill. If you were to leave my parents' apartment and travel down those narrow curving stairs, walk straight through the central cobblestoned courtyard of the genteel old building, pull the brass latch, and walk out the front door, you would find yourself looking down onto a slender street, hosting a few small shops and cafés. This street of mine, abetted by the force of gravity, insisted that you follow it, and when you did you would be led along a cobbled tributary down to the city's central artery. The river had broad banks lined by lindens, bending toward the water, providing shade for the lovers, painters, fishermen, and vagrants who populated its banks. Five bridges spanned the river, all made of stone. The bridge that extended off my street was the oldest of these, by hundreds of years, and the most famous, and it was lined on both sides by large marble statues of saints and warriors. Every week [this was before the statues were defaced, and pulled down, and before charges had been set and detonated, and the entire bridge demolished], my parents and I would walk down the hill to the market, and once our bags were full, we would continue out across this bridge. I remember now that I would sit on one of the bridge's many stone benches and feed the sparrows and starlings from a bag of crumbs or a tin of meat—brought expressly for this purpose—while my mother and father would walk over to the stone balustrade, lean up against it, his arm around her waist, and they would look out over the city's bustling waterfront, and watch the seabirds bob like buoys, and the broad river break up against the bridge's ice guards. Eventually, I would become bored, and shout over to my parents, who would turn toward me, looking like a pair of misbehaving children who had been caught out. My mother would peck my father on his rough cheek, and they would collect me. We would continue walking, maybe stopping at one of the vendors selling . . . [I don't know . . . chestnuts, spun sugar?]. The bridge let out on the far side of the river at a broad gravel park, fronting the porch of the city's basilica.

(I recall us, going up the steps, walking under the arches and through the tall doors, craning in the incense-filled space to see its distant ceiling. The basilica would have been lit up red, green, and yellow from the colored glass, which threw tinted specters around the vaults. There would have been reverberating silence; so quiet it would almost hurt my ears! We would walk, my mother and father holding hands, up the aisle to the front, until we were directly under the great round window, and then we would sit in silence and pray, while I fidgeted. On one particular morning, during which I had been beside myself with agitation [due to being made to sit quietly for so long, but also due to the astonishing fact of having been kissed by a girl—my first kiss, which had taken place just the day before, in the vestibule of the home of a red-haired girl I was courting], I ignored the sermon, and watched the citizens of the cathedral ambling in and among the chapels, around the back of the main altar, pointing out architectural elements to one another, breathing in the incense. It seemed to me then as if the basilica were a city-within-a-city, with its own avenues, and dead ends, resting spots, its duties and pleasures, its rituals and labors, its own toll plaza in the form of an old man taking admittance tickets; its economy of tithing boxes and candles and indulgences for sale; with a hierarchy of souls, the most elite of which presided, as in an actual city, high up, in this case way above, in the luminous color of the windows; ranks of martyrs, prophets, and emperors, looking down, stern, on a terrestrial population. Following their gaze, I looked down again, myself. My parents had resumed their prayers. I also bent my head to pray, but couldn't. All I could think of was my red-haired girl, and her lips; her smell. My mother looked over and up at me, I blushed, and she looked at me quizzically, then, smiling, gave me a little nudge. I nodded, and pretended to pray again. She bowed her head.

(We would walk back again, over the same bridge.

(It had been like this.)

The delivery boy pedaled.

Coasted.

Breathed deep.

The bridge smelled pungent. Oil, exhaust. Also:
1. Brackish smells (that would be the mudflats). Then:
2. The slightly rancid, weedy, cedar-like scent of the sea coming up the estuary. It hit him high in the nose, between his eyes. And: 3. Fresh air, swinging down out of the heights.

Such smells; such space. The bridge like some mythical colossus.

Cars thrummed past him. The road shook with the weight of the larger trucks.

He was on the upper deck, on the bridge's highest level, a fair bit past the first anchorage, three-quarters of the way up the approach ramp, nearing a green metal tower, which, arching back, he could see was as tall, at least, as the Royal Arms apartments, and strung like a maypole with what had to be hundreds of cables, each thicker than his waist. It was lavishly, gigantically arched, and everything was streaming through its aperture in a single direction, as if humankind itself were being welcomed in to some ultimate service, through the portico of some eternal hereafter. He stuck as close to the guardrail as possible, cars cannoning by, the wind pushing, in gusts, hard upon one side of his bicycle.

Having scanned the lane ahead, and checked the rear-view, he then risked a quick but full glance behind him. He saw the city, his city. A long, denticulate comb of buildings, rising dark against the world. Behind the city lay another city, built of cloud. He realized that the slope was easing and he was cresting the rise; just about flat again, so he turned to face forward, and saw then that he had reached the shadow of the tower, then was beneath it, then was through it, and then he was levitating, high above the river.

He stopped. Planted a foot down. The wind stung, but the sun shone. Down below: The scarred waters of the city's main waterway. Long and wide. From this new vantage, he could follow its course up and north, dotted with bright sails, leeched by dark barges. One stunning red tanker, caught out by the sun, a shining and beautiful toy. Where the river bent, far up ahead, the landscape greened dramatically. This would be Manor Grove, the delivery boy realized. Far to go, but not that far. In sight, that is.

I am doing it. I am doing it.

(And he truly was.)

At that moment, bicyclists, resplendent in bright-colored tights and sleek helmets swarmed by at startling speed.

"On your right!" someone hollered over their shoulder. Once again, it was too late to be a warning, and was most likely a reprimand. (Fuckers.)

And then the downward slope.

————————

The far side of the bridge led toward a toll plaza, which opened up onto a cliff face, atop which was a green area, a municipal park of some sort. This looked, from the bridge's deck, like a large sponge. It had none of a city's edges or angles. The traffic slowed, then stopped. Cars were lining up to pay an entry (or exit) fee at a row of tollbooths, which seemed to the delivery boy like the starting gate of some great, mechanical horse race. And after waiting—first behind a truck, then a family auto-mobile that featured a rear rack full of small bicycles—he slunk out of his lane, into another. He left that lane as well, and moved in this manner until he was around to the rightmost side of the traffic, and the farthest end of the plaza.

He debarked in front of a small storage shed. There was a flagpole, and a flag, which bore a mysterious em-blem and legend. The halyard pinged brightly against the metal of the pole. Next to this was a low concrete bunker with two doors, one of which was labeled: MEN (BOYS SHOWER HERE). He chained the bike to the flagpole, and went into the lavatory. The floors were wet from the storm earlier, or from a burst pipe, and he had to tread carefully around the archipelago of puddles to keep his shoes dry. He pissed over at the porcelain wall, then went to a stall and gathered toilet paper around his hand. Then to the sink. He turned it on, and quite surprisingly, hot water came out in a steady flow. He carefully reopened the tear in his pants, and examined the wound, which was redder around the edges than before, the cut itself angrier, and beginning to cake. He pinched the cut, and more blood came out, which he dabbed at with the toilet paper until it seemed relatively clean, then applied more paper as a kind of sticking plaster. Satisfied, he tied up the rip, stood, and cradled his hands under the tap to wash them, and to splash some water on his face. Then he looked up into the aluminum mirror, and saw himself.

His big cheeks were splotchy. His eyes were dark, his dripping brow heavier than normal in the low light. He considered his mouth, its thinness. He looked around him. MEN. He turned back to the mirror, and turned his head three-quarters. "Delivery man," he posited to the mirror. At that moment, a stall door banged open, and someone in a suit emerged. He walked to an adjacent sink, and began looping and tightening up his necktie, wincing as he did so, as if in pain. Then the man turned, and noticed the delivery boy before shaking his head disappointedly, taking one last look at himself, and walking out of the lavatory (without, the delivery boy noticed, having washed his hands). What must I look like now, the delivery boy thought. He looked at his own face, dripping, his hair sticking straight up, his ragged, sooty clothes. He cranked the lever on the towel machine, which brayed like a mule, but yielded nothing.

He walked out, wiping his hands on his pants.

In the lot: people. There were no delivery boys out on toll plazas, in the banlieues, on highways. He must seem to those in the cars and around the plaza like a victim of some sort; or worse, a lunatic. Outside the grammar of city life. ("*Fish out of water*: it means weirdo," N. had explained.) People loitered in the parking area, lingered by their cars, every eye seemed to assess him. Given his outlandishness to the people around him, he would need to proceed carefully; not to arouse attention and suspicion. It occurred to him then that there might be police around the toll plaza.

Police. He had not anticipated this, but of course they would be here. In all of his time in the city he had never had a problem with police. Never spoken to police, or been spoken to by police. He had been good always, obedient, at least when it came to traffic and rules. But if the policemen saw him here, they would question him (and why wouldn't they question him, why wouldn't they ask the strange, reedy boy-man—so clearly a refu-gee from the inner city—where he was heading and what he was carrying?). The bags, that is. The bags. And his mind flicked over to the bags, heavy on the bike's handlebars. He had left the bags with the bike. He had left the bags with the bike! Oh—

They were still there. But he would need to be more cautious from now on. What had he been thinking? He hadn't been. (It astounded him now, in the aftershock of panic, that he could ever have been so stupid as to have left the bags in this way. What if someone took them? And if someone had come along and taken the bags, what if they looked inside; what would they have found? His mysterious cargo.) He looked down at the laden bi-cycle. He passed a clinical glance over the bags. He felt a deep urge to reach into one of them and just . . . A look. One look. Who would know? Out here? The thought prompted him to peer around. No one was watching him. Cars inched forward and were released through the booths in a kind of listless rhythm, drivers focused on the road ahead. No one came in or out of the rest-rooms. He snatched a bag off the bike, lifted it, tried its weight. He put it down on the pavement and prodded it with a finger. It was clearly double- or triple-bagged, and his poke didn't yield much information. He tested the knot at the top of the bag, where its handles had been interlocked and pulled tight. Too snug to undo. He would have to rip or otherwise cut into it if he wanted to see inside. He knelt down, leaned over, and brought his face up close to the plastic. He could not see inside. He sniffed it. Nothing. Smelled like a plastic bag. He got up and walked in a circle once around the bag, thinking about cracking into it, next steps, and just then his phone buzzed.

N.'s number on it. A message:

—he asks u there yet

(And I will imagine her adding, perhaps, a note of concern—for the bags of course—but, as read here by the delivery boy, concern for his welfare, concern for his own person. Something like . . .)

—hurry

(Such that, then he might believe) it was as if she had known; known that he would be tempted. By the bags. She knew. Always seemed to know, and tenderness welled up in him, ran into the fear, diluting it. He flicked the phone off.

The delivery boy gave each of his legs a shake, regulated his thoughts, crouched again, unlocked the bike with rapid if still-shaking hands (hands shaking from newly inflamed ardor, adrenaline, fear . . . who knows), stood, and pushed out.

———————

He was breathing in big gusts. Many of the vehicles he had pedaled around in that crowded toll plaza now blurred past him, disappearing behind the curve ahead. As more went by, he tried to compensate for the drafts they left behind by leaning toward them. He kept his head low to avoid getting dirt in his eyes. He was cleaving so close to the shoulder of the road that his right ankle brushed continually, over and over, against the wet grasses and weeds alongside it. He was pedaling, yes, giving the mechanism another breather. Now, even when not in use, he could feel its troubling heat. So he pedaled and pedaled. And exhaustion fell over him like a blanket, yet he recognized that he could not flag; least of all now; not when he was so close. So he thrust forward, a marathon runner, a polar explorer (a soldier). He bent his head to the work, subordinated his entire being to the task, and did not look up again for another long period, perhaps hundreds of pedal-lengths long, hundreds of occasions where the wet grass teased at him; hundreds of whimpers, wheezes; hundreds of moments of discomfort and pain. He worked his way onward past a series of chain motels (vacancies) and petrol stations (self-serve) and cheap roadside eateries (shuttered), passing way markers that measured distance in a language of colorful squares and red stripes, like small nautical flags. A large (yellow) school bus came alongside him then, its tires tossing pebbles. It slowed in traffic, and a bunch of schoolboys released the catches on their windows to yell at him. He looked steadfastly forward as they did so. Then the traffic thinned and the bus pulled out. He could hear the laughter cut off abruptly by the closing windows. Another car came up, and someone threw a can. Later, a flicked cigarette arced by. He watched it bounce once, spraying embers onto the shoulder and landing in the grass. Farther on, there was the body of a large brown-striped animal in the breakdown lane. The body was flattened, large gashes running up both of its sides, revealing the meat, red, within. Flies had gathered. He steered around it, looking away, and then he looked down again. (He had seen two examples of such an animal, looking out guardedly from the branches of a scrub pine in an old zoo back in his homeland. The conductor had taken them there for a school outing, and, as they wandered between the cages, the girl with the French horn had held the delivery boy's hand. One of her fingers had curled, and tickled his palm. Her hand had been surprisingly small, light, and dry. The nail, a bit sharp. The delivery boy hadn't known whether she had curled her finger on purpose, but he didn't want to even breathe, lest she remove it. The conductor had lectured on the animals' countries of origin. He had also insisted that they visit the bird pavilion, so that he might notate their songs on a large pad of staff paper. They brought lunch in bags, as the food vendors had all been shuttered. No one wore a badge on their lapel anymore, by the time of that outing, and many of the fanciest animals had been removed from the zoo altogether. The ones that remained were common, and seemed sickly, wary.)

When, later, the delivery boy looked up, he saw a green road sign, which, as it grew, became legible: MANOR GROVE. He stood up out of his saddle and dove forward. Then the exit itself appeared out of a long bend, and he took it, coasting, then, down its generous curving hill (the choreography implicit in the setting perhaps reminded the delivery boy of the formal dances held long ago on the marble floor of the old public hall . . . except that, no, I am wrong: he was much too tired for nostalgia at this point) and the exit bottomed out at an empty intersection with a traffic light—red— a red that was beyond meaningless (and indeed meant something different out there in that district: that one was still allowed to turn), and without waiting to look even to see if there was oncoming traffic, he swung right onto the new access road, stopping only once on the shoulder, to wipe off the screen of his device with his sleeve, and retape the device to the handlebars; and he followed the map toward his destination, and then, around him, the streetlamps clicked on.

The road meandered through a gentle valley. As he rode, the scenery became more refined. The trunks—

leafless, wormy with vines—that bordered the highway stood straighter then, as if waking from a disordered rest. The air was softer, blurrier, and smelled of pine and wet fern (and it was quiet enough then that the delivery boy could have attended to the prosody of his bike: its whirs and clicks, catches and releases. Instead he listened to the wordless yet frightened and hectoring voice in his mind, which quoted without acknowledgment from the sound of the tires on the road: *Nnnnnnnn* . . .). For a period, a small, rocky stream ran a parallel course on his right. Then he saw his first mailbox (his first mailbox like this one, ever). Then another. So on. Driveways that disappeared into the woods. More roads like these. Then the road became bordered, on both sides, by wide lawns. Then more trees. Then the lawns again, some of these fronted by enormous and ornate entrances, gates with names written on them in wrought iron (1. *Winnecock.* 2. *Shadewoods.* 3. *Blighton* . . .), large hedge arches, or guardhouses—sometimes twin guardhouses on either side of a gravel entrance, these paths leading through boxwoods and privets (a few had long allées of sycamore or elm) to the portes cocheres and roundabouts of the largest houses the delivery boy had ever seen.

The mansions of Manor Grove. Elaborately roofed, gabled, turreted; girdled with balustrades, moated with meticulous shrubs. He tried not to gawk, to resemble too closely the robber or refugee he surely looked like. He hunched over as low as he could, and leaned in for another push.

Farther on.

    (Farther still.)

    He alternated pedaling and coasting. Pedaling and coasting. The estates swam past. While coasting, he pulled out his phone. Looked down, and then up, very quickly. No cars on the road. No obstacles. He passed a squat stone cycloptic country church that sat upon a small rise like a toad. It followed him with its single eye. The delivery boy remembered (and this memory took no longer than a moment; was over before he knew it had even occurred) another outing to a church, in his homeland: the conductor had taken them there for an organ recital, and the delivery boy recalled how, suddenly, the quiet of the sacred space had been obliterated by sound; how the congregants had all looked up. Those bright echoes. As the children in the orchestra listened to the fugue unspool, the delivery boy had been struck by the instrument's capaciousness: how it was entirely all-encompassing and self-sufficient; which is to say that an organ could be, as needed, a flute or a trumpet or a siren; whisper, idyll, explosion . . . (Whereas I am, now, more attuned to the fact that a fugue—any fugue—contains, packed within its preliminary notes, the hereditary material for every note that follows. The conductor may have, on that same day perhaps, imparted this same lesson about fugues to his young pupils; but I don't know for sure. In any case, the music had ended, and when it did, the delivery boy heard the notes hang in that vast space like particles of dust.)

———————

He pulled over then, between two roadside trees, hidden behind one of their enormous trunks, which he leaned his bicycle up against.

On the map, there were no blocks, but rather rough patches of land, divided unevenly like jigsaw pieces by access ways and private roads. He saw that he was almost there. Almost. He saw his destination, a small red pin spiked into the background at the end of what looked like a small cul-de-sac. So close.

He heard a bird call above him; a crazily melismatic and ornamented aria. Another bird, deeper in the copse behind, responded in similar, if paler fashion. He savored it. This moment. It was not a moment to let pass without ceremony. At least without some recognition of its importance. (The conductor would tell them to take big breaths at such times—to prepare for the stresses and stimulations of big finales; "Crescendos," he would say, "always begin quietly. This should go without saying, as this is how crescendos are marked. *Piano*, first, rising to *forte*. But when we see such a marking, our first inclination is to play loudly. Immediately loud. It is always true. Given this knowledge—this foreknowledge—that there is something big coming, we anticipate, then jump the gun. I don't know why. But it isn't your fault. It is human nature. But we may also be trained out of this habit. What I would like to teach you now, is that when you see the word *crescendo*, it means, in fact, *play quietly*.")

The air smelled of lavender and lawns. A sprinkler somewhere was whirring. Clouds of midges haunted the roadside like preying spirits. He lingered. The sun was still in the sky, but behind the trees, so that everything was shadow but the sky itself. Like the day was struck in two, and night and day coexisted. Single yellow beams broke through in places, glinting and ricocheting off wet greenery.

The delivery boy heard a car go by, slow, and crunch onto gravel, hundreds of yards away. The birds went silent. A transformer buzzed overhead. The sky, which, for the last hour, had been arrested in a state of reddening suspense, now yielded to darker shades, giving the feeling of an encroaching end. He thought of N. and once again wanted to message her. To say, *I made it.*

He stretched instead, bending over his feet, arching his back, pulling a leg back behind him.

A low rumble, which grew louder. Then a row of open-backed trucks went past, carrying equipment for cutting grass, trimming leaves. Workers in rough clothes crowded into the cabs, squatting alongside the machines, or sitting on the flatbeds, their legs dangling over the sides. A line of these trucks, like a parade. No one seemed to notice him there among the trees.

He waited, then they were gone.

It was the end of the shift.

Time. For him as well. He scratched an ear. Vigorously rubbed his face. Let out a little whistle. Then the delivery boy hopped back on his bicycle, smiling.

He'd pedal the last bit. He'd always known this was how the last leg would go. It would be triumphant. And he would be like a Thoroughbred, rounding the lathering final lap. As he pushed off onto the road, he heard a wail, stopped, pushed the bike with both feet until it and he were behind the tree again, and then he waited. The wail grew louder, and he saw the red flashing light wash over the street before him, and then the police car screamed by him. He winced at the noise. Then it rounded the corner and was gone, leaving a fading contrail of siren behind it.

Satisfied that it was finally safe, he rolled on.

The road meandered. There were no other cars. This

was now, truly, the countryside. The first he had seen of anything this rural since before the vessel. Forest. Fields, cordoned off by rustic wooden railings. Wildflowers. A silo poking up near the top of a gentle hill. A stand of birch, contravening the dark. Pockets of wet and heavy silence. Cicadas, in electric phases. No more sirens (though I can imagine the police waiting for him at his destination. Waiting with cuffs, and truncheons).

He biked faster, and at a bend in the road, something emerged, which resolved into a street sign. He slowed his bike, to ensure that the road was the correct one. Satisfied, he pulled off to his left onto a country lane, and pedaled to where the pavement, abruptly, ended. Trees picketing the dirt road on both sides, an orchard, a dirt road penetrating its heart. No more numbers. No houses. Yet he was so close now. His phone was chirruping the fact. His breathing grew more shallow. He looked around, and saw nothing. (He had pictured, in his mind, at the beginning of the delivery, it ending at an impressive, gated mansion at the end of a long road. The approach was to be a processional. A victory march; full of pomp.) He pedaled on, though traction was difficult. Small, prune-ish apples lay scattered along the roadside. The road began to narrow, further, and further still. It was now a mere path, not wider than a city bicycle path. This, he thought—allowing, for the first time, his sunken suspicions to surface a bit—was worrisome, and he took a single hand off the handlebars and felt his collar. Damp. The bike lurched on a rock, he put both hands back on. The trees merged in toward him. A branch stung him; he ducked, still pedaling. Another branch. It swiped at his arm. Another. The sound of crickets merged with the growling of his tires. Every muscle complained. The ground grew more and more uneven. He peered forward, and then he saw something up ahead. This would be it. Had to be. A fence post, barely visible in the vesperal gloom. He slowed. Approached. A log lay across his path, fronting a wall of green. It was the end of the road at last.

And there was nothing there.

CHAPTER THIRTY-FOUR

The delivery boy peered into the darkening orchard, and saw

(A picnic.)

(No.)

(Sorry.)

(That doesn't go here.)

(But still.)

(It was the fall, and I was with my parents. Beer foam on my mother's upper lip . . . She wiped it away, cross, then amused. My father, and his walking stick, knobby like a pretzel, its pommel worn smooth. A scratched metal compass; a waxen map. We bent over it. His hands . . . fluvial veined, mountainously knuckled . . . I kicked rocks down the road . . . ferns, patches of fringed and elaborately vented mushrooms in between tree roots . . . A climb, a clearing, the sun, a view, the return . . . the orchard again . . . the darkening orchard . . . and then . . . no.)

(There is no picnic here. It's gone.)

———

The delivery boy peered into the darkening orchard, reached for his phone, and double-checked the address.

There it was: the pin on his phone's map. Right next to it: a throbbing dot. He was there. Here, he thought, enlarging the scene until it was clear that the dot was right next to the pin. The customer must be *here*. This was the place. Yet, it could not be. He turned a full circle. He squinted. He said a tentative hello to the murk, knowing as he did so that it was futile. He read through all his texts again to see if he had missed anything, periodically stopping to swat a bug. It all seemed correct, yet clearly was not. Panic rising, he stood astride his bicycle, the chain heavy on his chest, his leg stinging, the sweat evaporating uncomfortably from his cool forehead. The handles of the doubled plastic bags were stretched thin. He got off. Maybe, just maybe, his destination, his customer—the Supervisor's *special* customer—lived off the road? Beyond this dark copse, maybe just over that rise? He thought he had seen the vestiges of a trail, and so he wheeled his bicycle, stepping between trees, walking it, the tires bumping along the rock- and root-covered ground—as foreign a movement for him after his long ride as that of stepping onto a swaying vessel. The hill became steeper, the undergrowth denser, the terrain rockier, and the delivery boy knew that he would need to carry his bike. It seemed wrong, carrying the bike that carried the bags (a violation of natural law: the conveyance conveyed, a transitive delivery), but he had no choice. So he lifted it. Slightly; experimentally. The power-assist was heavy, as was the bicycle itself (not to mention the bags on its handlebars). He bent his knees low, and endeavored to jerk the bike upward like a weight lifter. It took him several spastic attempts to get it up onto his shoulder, but eventually he succeeded. He stood there for a moment, breathing heavily, the crossbar digging into his clavicle uncomfortably. He swayed a little on his feet. Then he began to trudge. One foot after the other. The mud squelched and sank a bit under his weight. It was heavy going, and he had to stop frequently to lean on a tree and catch his breath. His legs were shaking. He reached firmer ground, larger rocks. Steeper. Low branches investigated the spokes of his tires, and he had to yank the bicycle free, tiring him further. Still, despite the huge effort it cost him, he managed it; he endured, portaging in this manner until he was up and over the hill, where he stopped, heaved the bicycle up, and released it back down, leaning it up against a trunk. He looked about him again. The view was wide, if dark. He saw more trees in all directions. Somewhere in the distance, the orchard gave way to real wilderness, with its higher, spikier skyline. Beyond and far down below there was a glint of light on what looked like a meandering river. But no lights, no buildings, no sign of people.

This could not be right. None of this was right.

He felt tears begin to rise.

He looked at his phone again.

Then he thumbed:

—nothing here

Then:

—*address wrong*

He slumped down onto the mossy ground, crossed his legs. The device sat mute on his lap. He powered it on again, it died again. He went through this process again, and again. Then he texted:

—no address

And again:

—NOTHING HERE.

And:

—where do I go

Then:

—what do I do (what do I do what do I do)

Finally:

—??????

All thought of being a man about things fled. He no longer cared about appearances (as on the vessel, the situation had abolished questions of pride or shame). His throat hurt. He imagined the Supervisor asking questions; the interrogation of N., in his office, the door barred; an interrogation over the bags; the delivery boy's whereabouts. He imagined the Supervisor's patience snapping like a toothpick in that rotted and muscular mouth. He thought of N. trying to be a tough nut through it all. *But how tough a nut could someone be?* He could only hear the branches stirring, and the sound of his own panting. He drooped behind the branches and could smell the sour apples, putrid beneath him. The mosquitoes were out. He swatted more of them. The wind picked up again, and the mosquitoes went away along with the fireflies. The thought of returning to the city in the night made him ill. Still, he rose, checked the bicycle's condition, using the dim yellow glow from his weakening flashlight. The diminishing beam made the bike look ugly, and vaguely sinister. The frame was splattered with dirt and mud. Shreds of plastic bag hung from the frame where they had been taped, like ghostly shrouds. Some of the spokes had been bent. In the spot where he usually kept his water bottle there was nothing at all. The power-assist was hanging at a strange angle. He thumbed its switch to no avail. The mechanism did not heat up, grind, or even make a sound; it was as dead as could be. Dead and ineffectual as he, himself. He slumped again to the ground. After some moments, he grabbed his hair, pulled, and winced. He took a deep breath as if to scream but let out no detectable noise. What could he do?

Perhaps find shelter? He had seen a barn, back on the road. A sinister, listing structure, abutting a large field, stubble in the colorless dusk. There had been a large midden of hay and rags. A scarecrow. Bleak, and, no, it was too far back now. He knew, rejecting this option, that he would not be getting back on the bike at all that night.

Branches in the wind.

He listened, fearful, working to distinguish the breaks in those treacherous woodland noises, to tease certain sounds out from the general pastoral hum, groan, and chirp, to distinguish the natural from the unnatural, the crack of the larger trees in the wind from the snap of a twig that has been stepped upon, the wood's dimpled boles from faces, branches from arms, the gossiping leaves from whispers.

He looked up, only to see a sliver of bright light, which was a broken fragment of the moon itself, rising up in the interwoven orchard, haloing each branch with subtle irradiation.

Night. Night was a fact now. (A fact. Indisputable. An undeniable state of affairs.)

He turned on the phone again: 10 percent. No messages.

His mind stuttered, unable to translate the world as it stood. He looked at the bags, and finally admitted that they were all that he had now; that he was otherwise on his own, and that no matter what was within them, they were his lot, his burden, his riddle, his path, from here on out. Yet whatever was to be done with them, he decided that it could not be done now; so he placed the bags in a pile up against a large tree trunk, and covered them in leaves, covering that pile with his bike. He checked his phone one last time and turned it off to conserve the slim remainder of its battery. He pulled his thin jacket tight around him, pulled his knees up to his chest, and lay down on his side.

He felt again as if he would cry, and then tried to—screwing up his features, though he knew this was false. He fought a palpable sense of erasure, a kind of bleaching of his essence; as of the pale highlight on a wall after a piece of furniture of long standing has been removed. (*Who was he now, in these parlous circumstances?* I ask myself this question, about the delivery boy, just as he asks the same question, using different words, about himself.)

He had no answers. He looked around, then up at the sky (and, my sincere apologies, but memories do not obey propriety, or context, or anything, really, except for the prompts of their own mysterious summons, such that I now recall another dark sky, seen from just such a field, how it was suddenly filled with the phosphorescent lines of tracers, seeking out some distant plane, as if a host of shooting stars had suddenly reversed direction . . . such wonders . . . and now, just like that the image passes), though the delivery boy's stars remained fixed in place

★★★, etc.

. . . and he constellated them in different ways . . .

. . . but it came to him that each of these lights might represent only a trace of a celestial body perhaps long gone and only that—a vestige of cosmic memory—and so, needing to calm himself differently, and further, he counted: 1, 2, 3, 4 . . .

His breathing slowed. The wind was subsiding. A firefly scripted past his knee. Another hovered nearby. A rich smell of dirt. He stretched a leg, relaxed it. Drew his hands under his head to make a pillow.

Then he asked himself (and answered) simple questions in his new language.

1. "How many packages?"
2. "What floor?"
3. "Can you sign this?"

N.

He thought through forms and cases.

N.

He thought of N., he thought of her: *upon*; *atop; beside; under; around; above*; before; with; through; since; across; after; (and most difficult of all) *beyond.*

He thought of all the varieties of *to be* that he could remember, but kept, as ever, being pulled, cold and thrashing, into *is.*

N.

He considered that the world felt strange, as if it had committed a solecism, and that any action he might take henceforth would be declined as an irregular verb might.

He tried the past again; he forced the tense. He pushed at it insistently, declining and declining, until at last, he landed, and stepped onto its reluctant and receding banks, safe; though undeniably emigrant.

CHAPTER THIRTY-FIVE

(Little rumblings, which you'd have to have been listening for to hear. My parents' friends sitting at the dining table, their efforts at keeping voices low. Fragments of a hushed argument. About staying or leaving. About what to do, and when to do it. Later, sounds of dishes being washed—the intimate tones of my parents, alone again, under the sounds of clanking tableware. *Maybe they were right*, my mother was saying, repeating it then: *Maybe they were right.* My father saying something equally vehement, failing to calm her. Sometimes I would walk down the dark, picture-lined corridor to my parents' bedroom to ask a question, and would hear, through the door: *Soon*; or: *We need to be ready*; or: *The time is now.* Then I would knock, and my father would answer, pulling his suspenders back up again, taut over his undershirt. My mother would be standing on the far side of the room, flushed with what was clearly anger. My father would gently steer me off, take me to bed, his hand warm on the small of my back, me having forgotten to ask whatever question I had concocted as an excuse to interrupt.

(I knew about the meetings my mother had just begun to attend because I had seen the pamphlets by the washing basin in the back of the apartment under some linen. I knew, and could picture, even then, the kerchiefs and caps, and now, from this vantage even further removed, I can hear the speeches given, blocs formed, positions seconded, or mooted, manifestos signed, pledges inducted, bright futures foretold; I see the men, coarse and barreling, sweat-slicked hair, the women's strong hands, fervent gestures, merry eyes, all of these peasants, scholars, schoolmasters, union organizers, *feuilletonists*, rebel priests, fallen patriarchs, utopianists, underground letterpress operators, railway and steelworks picketers, rabble-rousers, *agents saboteurs*, samizdat poets, that miscellany that embraced my charismatic—if schismatic and quarrelsome—mother as one of their own, and there were, naturally, arguments between my parents about the meetings, though always conspiratorially subdued. One night my mother came home much later than usual. My father had been pacing the apartment, fumigating it with worry and pipe smoke. I had watched him sit in the dining room, place his forehead down, gently on the table, light flickering around him on the polish of the dark wood. I saw him rise, pull his beard; sit, try to read, push the book aside; get up again and make some phone calls. More pacing. When my mother finally came back in, late in the night, she looked at my father as if from a height, her gaze running down her long, elegant nose—imperturbable, defiant, like a woman whose second might be standing just offstage with a monogrammed box of dueling pistols—and my father approached her warily, stuttered, but then embraced her out in that thin, yellow glow of the entrance hall, and her posture softened, all her fight fled, as she slumped into his arms. Like this. Things like this. Signs, barely legible. Just the littlest things, really. For instance, getting to school some mornings became more difficult because of manifestations in the city center, and I had to take my bicycle on a longer, hillier route, just to avoid it all. [Yes, I most certainly owned a bicycle back then. That bike had been red, presumably bright once, but dulled with heavy use. It had a scratched chrome headlamp, detailed fenders, and leather paniers, which I had received as a saint-day present from my father. I kept my schoolbooks and sports uniform in the bags, and my overcoat lashed to the rear rack. I rode this bicycle all around the city, until it became dangerous to do so on any and every route.] And then I began to hear—in the middle of, say, a history class, as the teacher's hand was poised above the chalkboard—sirens. More and more of them. [These sirens were different from the sirens I hear now, in this adoptive country of mine. The old sirens were hand-cranked, and described the interval of a fifth, like the open strings of a fiddle—this fifth perpetually melting away, tones losing coherence, the interval becoming sloppy, and falling, forming—as the sirens would depart, veering off toward their victims—a diminished fifth.] But not only noises, silences also. Long periods of quiet: especially in the evenings, when things used to be at their most lively. All at once, the sounds I was accustomed to hearing from my pillow at night—tourists, vendors, drunks, revs and tire shrieks [and seeing accompanying lights] from the passing cars, the ruffling pigeons, the lone dog barks—all gone. At this point my parents had taken to speaking to each other *only* in their bedroom, only very late at night, and only with the radio playing [in a register that, in music, we might call—rather musically—*mur-mu-rando*], and I could hear the hum of these conversations, just over the music, which they would put on at low volume, so everything blended into a single [well, it was actually more of a feeling, but also] hushed sound. My mother had begun writing at that point. Piles of paper began to accumulate in the house, covered with her mannish scrawl. I did not investigate further [having other concerns], and so did not know what it was she had been working on, but knew that she took to her task with an intensity that was only matched by my father's discomfiture at her doing so.

(So, paper. And paper accumulated on the streets as well. Piles of it, swept to curbs, and into drains. And posters—wheat-pasted to buildings and newspaper kiosks. One had been stuck up on a wall by my school. It pictured the corpulent and benevolent gaze of a large man wearing a military uniform, though also a peasant's tam. The entire tableau was jaunty and vaguely amusing, but, one morning, as we children filed into school, we saw that there was a slogan, newly, sloppily painted directly over it [and him]. We read the dripping words. It had been painted in the night. I understood the painted motto only vaguely, though the phrase—as well as the manner of its inscription—struck me, even with partial understanding, as brazenly contemporary, avant-garde, quite daring. It was visible from my classroom windows. We boys, in particular, were fascinated and aroused by it, such that we kept looking away from our teacher, craning to get a better view, keeping a kind of informal vigil over it, like boys do over a wild animal they've cornered—excited by its ferocity, but equally fearful. The graffiti lasted exactly three and one half hours into the school day. Several men came then with big brushes, and painted over the entire wall. Later, a squad of uniforms [along with a zealous pair of low-hipped dogs] descended on the school itself, and requisitioned the principal's office.

([Even later, I would hear my own mother repeat this controversial slogan, from the graffiti, say it as if she had coined it herself. It seemed, at first—despite the conviction with which it was said—as alien a thing to emerge from her mouth as a cloud of bees; though upon reflection, I should not have been as taken aback by this as I was.]

(Little rumblings. Yes, but then, then one night, I had been lying on my stomach on the great reading-room rug in our apartment [as all of the tables and chairs were covered with my mother's papers], and I had been just on the verge of finishing my schoolbook assignments when the first few loud knocks came on the door. The feeling was as if someone had shaken our home like a toy box. No furniture jumped, nothing overturned. No plaster dust snowed down from the ceiling. But still, I had the sense of life itself having leapt to some adjacency. I felt that, as of this exact juncture, my narrative would now be heading out in a completely other, new direction, along a new line. It was not real. It did not feel real, these knocks [which were really more thumps; the sounds made by a strong, determined, but gloved hand; the hand of someone backed by, and clothed in the apparatus of state], and then the second set of knocks hit the door, and then more, and I heard loud voices in the corridor; and as my parents scattered, snatching up my mother's papers that littered the apartment, I thought: It isn't real, it can't be. [This bit is difficult; difficult, even now, to discuss, and perhaps one shouldn't discuss it, as one can't—and perhaps one has no right to—convey the sheer otherness of such a world; when life is cast into ruin in such a manner; this is not, in some sense, even discussable, as this new life was not, in fact, representative of what we mean when we even say "life." This was an other-life, an anti-life, or another form of death. Now, I did not, then, think in such terms. Of course not. I was young, and I knew then only what I knew. These were mostly feelings instead of words— forbidding feelings—feelings that arise again in me now, and yet I dwell upon, strangely, most of all: the old, red bike—just the bike, only this now—and I wonder if it still exists somewhere; if it is being ridden by some-one, has been refurbished for some luckier child, or whether it lies rusted, in pieces in a culvert somewhere.] Either way, these were hard days, and they began, as they were bound to begin. And yet . . . one of the surpris-ing things to learn about such terrible times [and yet another example of how a general attempt to imagine the hardships of others is bound to fail] is that I did not find these hard times uniformly difficult. Of course there was—for me and my family, after the knocks on the door—pain, fear, and deprivation, but humanity [and life in general] has been known to adjust to every manner of wretchedness, and what might once have been considered unbearable in times of peace and pros-perity, may come to seem routine during protracted pe-riods of duress [this is especially true for children—who are malleable, and for whom every moment, no matter the context, is an exercise in uncertainty and estrangement]. But this is not exactly what I mean: I do not mean that I had become habituated to the new misery; I do not mean that my skin had thickened; or that I had, throughout these trying episodes, successfully learned to live on less, to eke out a smaller, meaner existence, which—because there had been no other choice—imposed a new means of measurement, which I would employ like a [broken] pair of calipers to determine my own relative happiness. No, what I intend to say is that there were important features of my life that, on occasion, superseded much of the suffering, notably, my upswelling adolescence, which was just beginning to exert itself then—a budding manhood that needed just such an upheaval as its proper context. That is to say, that the events that transpired after the officials had descended on my parents' apartment and swept up my mother's papers had become the outward confirmations of a tumult I already suffered. It had become clear to me that my story would necessarily be that of a lead actor, beset by hardship. Hardship, then, became the correct milieu for my having become romantically entangled, for instance, and after this, everything was from then on played out in front of an operatic backcloth; painted scenery backing a storybook drama. In just this way, we became the principal players in this theater—the girl with the red hair, who was my first heroine; and the fact of my having one then made all my other losses bearable. [And please don't imagine that I am being glib here; that I am in any way trying to diminish, or otherwise misrender my own suffering. But also: facts are facts.] Anyway, this state of affairs—my starring role in this world-historical romance of my own devising—lasted right up until our separation, and the first days of my voyage to this country, at which point all narrative was rendered meaningless and when the narrative fled, so did my ability to properly picture the girl I loved.

(When I sought her face in the intervening time, later, after we had parted, I found its image faded, as naturally it would be. But even at the beginning, believing that I could perhaps pin down her likeness with words, I began to think of ways to use language—my native tongue that is, the one in which we spoke together—to render and reanimate those features. I remembered that I had once thought her pretty, but then, there is a moment when, all at once, a word will suddenly seem wrong—woefully inappropriate—perhaps, in this case, the impoverishment of the word *pretty* occurred at the precise moment of our first intimacy—which had been so surprising, so beyond the realm of the possible, up until the instant it had occurred, that once it had, I knew the old words would not do anymore—and I remember [once] having considered newer words, more grown-up words, though these words also failed to tell this story properly, to summon her . . . So what about a detail, I thought then [as I think now; as specificity matters], but it is her pure and intoxicating quiddity that I cannot capture—though I remember inhaling from deep in her neck's lower hollows, our bodies meeting, our hands alert . . . [re "our bodies meeting": I feel inclined to remind you that it was all very chaste. Though, though: what is this *chaste*, really? Are the feelings and sensations we felt then, during this first embrace and its aftermath—a phantasmagoria of longing and confusion—could these feelings really be considered chaste? If so, then chastity is a sight more forceful, elemental than its opposite], but either way, either way, it is clear [to me, now] why I found such a solution to the problem of "capturing" the image of this girl of mine so problematic. It was because my version of her was then [and would be, henceforth] constructed entirely from my own material. She would provide nothing more. So perhaps [I thought once] it was the case that she could be evoked through a minute examination of these same feelings toward her; and if I only attended to my feelings closely enough she would emerge out of them. This also failed. It was an unfortunate fact that she was no longer contributing to this store of knowledge and so I was [and am, still] stuck with my own impoverished dictionary, my faded album of images, those compromised memories and dreams: all of these being lies of a sort. Furthermore [and to make matters more complicated], this accumulation of material concerning her had—without my having been made conscious of it—migrated away from the person herself, colonized other faces, become conflated with other experiences, smells, feelings, a new life, and so she merged with new people altogether, such that it is undeniable [to me, again, now] that personhood may be, actually, transferable [a tragic conclusion to come to], that in the face of memory's true extinctions, one prefers transfiguration—one thing seeping into, and replacing another; this being memory's [and empathy's] central, colonizing presumption—such that these collected experiences of ours would comprise not so much a dictionary of feeling, but rather a thesaurus [which every dictionary, at heart, is], and so, after all this, it had all—all of it: my parents, the strife, the girl I loved, and even the trip over [of which we will say less than nothing]—it had all become something new. Everything, every feeling, urge, thought, every chapter in my history [as with that of the delivery boy, bedded against those cold roots, in his shallow sleep beneath a tree] had been decanted into new containers.

([And not to bore you again with these refrains—having already bored you with so many interruptions—but the delivery boy, though he felt as I did in this regard, did not know the word *decanted* any more than he knew that this particular transferal of feeling had taken place for him; but now, as I sit up from my task and turn my gaze out my window to the treetops and to the river beyond, the phrase feels apt.] All of which is to say that the delivery boy spoke, as I myself now speak: an amputee language—a language in which whole tenses had been lopped off, a language of the present only—a language that subsequently required an even newer, supplementary, makeshift language; prosthetic, and ill-equipped for mourning.)

PART III

We can also imagine the case where nothing at all occurred in one's mind except that one suddenly said "Now I know how to go on."

CHAPTER THIRTY-SIX

(And here is how I would imagine it. Care to imagine it.)

(Should I not care?)

(Will I care wrongly?)

(Yes.)

(Yet still I would have the delivery boy waking up, and)

he had been dreaming, and, foggy as things were, he thought at first that perhaps he was dreaming still, the dream pertaining to a language lesson, a lesson given by N. in which she was presenting the delivery boy with a list of words for him to memorize, and he dreamed that he was repeating these words back to her, one at a time, phonetically (even in the dream he had realized that this language lesson was a fantasy; that this was not how these things went, or how they should go—of course not, he had said to himself, still in the dream), when the scene of the language lesson shuddered, and slipped, and then the delivery boy was sitting on a capstan, aft on some vessel, watching the churning swells emanating out from its screws—the cold, clean air whipping his *noix de coco* hair up, ruffling his thin, damp jacket; it was freezing out there, yet a feeling of boundless freedom was seeping in with the chill, a feeling of endless prospects on distant shores, and in the dream he laughed for joy, laughed at the promise of it all, but also laughed at the color of the sky, which was strangely beyond his ability to name, though obviously distinct (and distinctly obvious) especially when held up, as it was, to (above) the color of the sea (which was a deep green), and in the dream, the color's name continued to elude him, tease and confound him, and then he turned and saw the girl with the French horn, looking stiff, and sallow, standing in a kind of formal stance, the corners of her mouth turned up vaguely, as if posing for a long-exposure portrait; wearing her simple shift, a yellow badge affixed to her breast, a kerchief on her head, neither speaking nor moving (not even her eyes moved, not so much as a flicker), though the entire tableau rocked, slowly, silently, side to side in a sickening yaw, though he noticed, even in the dream, that she kept her footing, strangely untroubled by the precariousness of the pitching deck, and he felt himself wanting to pose questions, well, one question, namely a question concerning her whereabouts outside the dream (for he knew he was dreaming), meaning was she, even now, laboring at some other distribution center or warehouse (and surely he knew, seeing her in this vision that the answer to this question was certainly: no—and that

256

in fact she must lie, or drift along the bottom of some icy northern waterway, sunk down, below its lively waves, beneath the wavering keels of tankers and liners and barges like this one, below the trawlers' nets and strange swarms of life, and he imagined underwater cyes, and in them the murky reflection of a hull passing by, phantasmal, far, far overhead), and he stepped toward her and (as is the way of such things) it came to the delivery boy's attention that behind the spot where she stood—the center of the deck—something loomed up: a large mountain, a mountain-in-pieces, choppy and variegated, circled by cackling marine birds, a mountain of garbage perhaps; and as he grew nearer, he could suddenly see that it was made of bags and boxes, and, as he walked closer toward the forward slope, he saw that each box and bag was newly packed, clean, and clearly labeled, and so he approached closer, and began to walk up onto the pile, and as he climbed he bent down periodically to examine names and addresses, and slowly began to develop a theory, which was ultimately—in the dream, that is—borne out, as he began to recognize that the boat was charged with carrying not just any deliveries, but *his* deliveries; and, curiosity finally getting the better of him, he grabbed up a box indiscriminately, and began to tear at it, finding purchase with his fingernails on the stringy packing tape, which he tore away, and he pulled the flaps apart, and inside, wrapped

up in tissue paper, was a watch, an old one, like his older
brother's, the windup kind, no longer manufactured or
worn, which he stuffed into his breast pocket, then he
grabbed another package, and opened this one as well
(it contained a tinned ham, which he tossed aside) and
then a bag (French horn) and another (pad of paper;
pencils; India rubber eraser), and he worked his way in
this manner up through the lower slopes, keeping
what he wanted, dropping what he did not, his pockets
bulging, and indeed each and every bag of food, every
book, plant, every pet, every important document, every
game, tool, garment, weapon, lamp, toy, painting,
piece of scientific equipment, item of silverware, each
instrument, bottle of perfume, computer, bag of coffee,
orthopedic shoe, each bag of apples (there were a surprisingly large number of apples there), every pillow,
sewing machine, and Crock-Pot, every item he'd ever
been charged with carrying (and actually, also: would
ever have to carry) was here, in this pile, and he went
on, continued in such a manner, opening bag after
bag, box after box, one after another, until he was in a
kind of frenzy . . . but then, without ceremony, the
boat, and with it, the pile he was standing on, was
gone and the delivery boy was bobbing adrift, the distant horizon cutting the globe neatly in half in all directions, and the sea closed over him; and something
bit him; he swatted at his arm, rubbed it, and it began

to itch, and his eyes opened; after which he rose, confused, not knowing his own name, age, or whereabouts: and quite appropriately, mist was everywhere, curling around the trunks of the apple trees and his bicycle, sweeping down the orchard's hills, and his pants and jacket were damp, and he lurched up onto one arm, sat upright, rubbed his eyes, and he saw that the sun was busy ruddying the sky's pale complexion, while his lower back hurt terribly, and he looked down to see that he had slept on a thick, snaky root, and then he noticed the pain in his calf, and saw (because his pants had hiked up in the night) the wound, raw, which was when he remembered the chain of events that had brought him to this strange no-place, and the entire previous day, unreal as the nautical dream he had just awoken from, long as a century, wrought with fear and confusion; it rushed back to him, and he gasped, and scrambled up then toward the camouflaged bike: and thankfully, it was still where he had left it—the bags intact and unmolested—at which point, in a new spasm of fear, he reached into his pocket to grope for his phone, which he found, and removed, and he turned it back on, learning then that there was, miraculously, still a little bit of charge left, a single half bar of it, and looking around him as if to ensure a privacy that was wholly assured in the midst of the enormous orchard, he pressed the number for N. (it would be very early in the warehouse) and heard the phone ring—it was ringing—and (would anyone be awake yet?) then someone picked up. "Hello?" said the delivery boy, watching the small cloud of air leak from his mouth, then: 1. "I could not find the customer." But no one responded, so he said again: 2. "Hello?" And then: 3. "Please tell me what to do." And then: 4. "Is there anyone there?" And then: 5. "Nothing is here, and no one." But there was silence on the other end—not a dead silence, a voluminous silence, the silence of space, and of the almost sub-audible sounds of someone waiting in that space—and he spoke one more time, not probingly, but weakly, in defeat: 6. "Hello?" And (let us say—intervening once again on the delivery boy's behalf—that finally) a woman's voice answered: soft, quite difficult to hear, but distinct enough so that he could tell, immediately, that this was not N., that there was someone else entirely on the line, he knew that this someone had N.'s phone (someone, again: who wasn't her), and this other person (this non-N.) then spoke once more, saying: "Are you in the place?" To which the delivery boy replied, "Who is this? I think that I am in the place. I mean that I thought I was in the place." Then he repeated into the phone, "There is nothing here." And then again, "Who *is* this?" To which she replied: "Dispatch girl," then pausing before adding, "Girl number six." Dispatch girl number six being, in fact, someone who was familiar to the delivery boy, a person who he had seen often—manning the station next to N.'s, a quiet, heavyset person with a broad, speckled face (a rare gentle presence in the warehouse, a person who never made fun of the delivery boy, or yelled at him, or even looked at him sternly, one who looked the other way when the delivery boy had been lying on the mats under N.'s desk, when he had been hiding out in the warehouse without being able to work, who never had a bad word for anyone, but who also never really seemed to speak with anyone at all either, who kept her own counsel—though her small, shining eyes betrayed a surreptitious intelligence that, if not overtly demonstrated, seemed none the less vital—a person who could have been, for all that the delivery boy or anyone else had thought about her, another piece of warehouse furniture), but as the delivery boy was standing in that orchard, shivering with chill and fatigue, he spontaneously recalled incidents to which she was party, in which she was a principal (if supporting) actor, including a time when the delivery boy had seen N. speaking with this girl, dispatch girl six, off in a corner, and there must have been some form of—if not friendship—complicity between them, the two dispatch girls, and in fact, the delivery boy now distinctly recalled a specific moment when there had been a small electrical fire in the dispatch corridor, back behind the desks, where the power lines from all the machines—

which were connected to a bulbous outlet, routed with cords and cables, and which, overheated, had sizzled and burst briefly into bright flame, and N. had sworn bloody murder and another dispatch girl (mean dispatch girl number five, I think it was) had gone off half-cocked, and flapped, impotently, at the blaze with her clipboard (ill-advised, quite literally fanning the flame), while the dispatch girl next to N. (the dispatch girl in question, dispatch girl six) had, while everyone panicked, simply and unceremoniously grabbed up a handful of the cords and yanked them all at once out of the socket (like a root from the ground), effectively stopping the fire, and in the aftermath, in the fishy smell of the electrical blaze, while everyone was examining the damage to the carpet, N. had looked over admiringly at dispatch girl six, who was blushing and breathing heavily, not from the unusual exertion actually, but because she was on the larger side and breathed heavily even in a resting state, but the important thing was that the delivery boy thought that he had never seen N. like this before, exhibiting this particular look, that N. did not seem to admire anyone at all, and so this dispatch girl six was clearly, in N.'s eyes, a person of substance, and here she was: answering N.'s phone instead of N., and the delivery boy—dancing foot to foot in the cold morning—here he was: trying to figure out why, to puzzle it all out in those infinitesimal moments before he spoke again, and when he spoke, he said, "Where is she?" to which the other dispatch girl did not reply, and there was silence, punctuated only by creaking trunks and susurrating leaves, an occasional bird, but other than these rustlings of an empty world: nothing; and the clock froze, stock-still, and it was as if there were no further steps for the delivery boy—or anyone else, ever again— to take, no further need for planning or movement, for thought or feeling, as if life itself had become stuck, arrested, mechanism frozen, chain twisted off its gears, brakes locked, and he did not know how long it was that he stood there in that silence (though he could hear her soft, insistent breathing) among those twisted trees, on that hard ground, the icy phone pressed to his ear (but, though it felt like a lifetime, it could not have been very long, as his phone's battery was drained, almost to nothing), but before his device died completely he heard, as from a great distance, on the other end of the connection, the dispatch girl say, "Hey? *Still there?*" And he mumbled, "Yes," and she said, "Open the bags." (And here she stopped for another pause, and he could imagine her cupping the phone to whisper.) "She said to make sure that I told you to do what she says and not be a stupid idiot about it." And finally, "I'm going to go now, so, do you understand?" And the delivery boy, dumbfounded, responded, mechanically, before his mind had caught up with his mouth: "I should open the bags," and dispatch girl number six sighed a little, then said, very, very quietly, but just as resolutely: "Yes," and the connection abruptly went dead. He looked down at his phone, and saw the battery icon blinking, the phone having mere seconds left in its life, and knowing how far he was from anything, he might as well (he thought) just chuck the thing off into the bushes for all it was worth to him now, as ineffectual as a corpse, another drained body, another encumbrance in a lifetime of encumbrances, and then he looked up and around him, and saw that during the call to the warehouse he had wandered quite far from his tree, quite unconsciously, and that he was standing in a small clearing, a field of dewy clover, crabgrass, and dandelions (which I now recall may be eaten in dire circumstances, to stave off hunger, and I can taste the bitterness), and he felt a stab of pain in his gut, and remembered that it had been ages since he last ate properly, and his stomach churned for a moment, spasmed such that he thought he might have to sit down on the spot, and with this uncomfortable stirring in his gut there followed the further uncomfortable realization that he wasn't sure which direction his tree was anymore, oh fuck, the tree against which he had slept, and under which was buried those bags—the bags the Supervisor had compelled him to carry, which he had been told, categorically, were unopenable, and which, now, were not only made unaccountably available to him, but also seemed his last and only line to N., as if the bags contained within them all of *her* secrets, all of her mysteries, as if they were some kind of passage through time and space directly to her, wherever she was—and where *was* she now: red and yellow-green bruises rising, yet another beloved body the location of which was forever unknown to him; or, or: perhaps she might be on the run somewhere, attempting to stray beyond the reach of the Supervisor and the world of captivity and servitude he presided over and represented, meaning that, with some luck, she might (he hoped, fervently) be beyond the reach of him, of each and every Supervisor, and he wished this for her so strongly then that he (though he would not have called it this) was actually praying (something I have never managed to do), though the delivery boy had prayed before in other ways; he had told himself hopeful stories (and it is so hard for me to distinguish between a prayer—those prayers for ourselves as well as our prayers for others—and a certain type of story). For instance: "tales of the girl with the French horn," and in his young mind these stories, with their joyous conclusions, had been restorative and yet the idea that such a narrative might actually befall him eventually, and bring about such (visceral, actual) pain—not the abstract, imaginary, symbolic, or literary variety—pain that would grab his guts and double him over in some foreign field under these unfeeling and alien branches would have, of course, been unthinkable to his young self, but life does have a way of reiterating ideas, reprising them in different modalities and meanwhile, spinning in that field, stumbling around it like a drunk, trying to retrace his steps back to the tree; and there were just so many of them, trees, all of them looking the same, but there *was* a trace of something, just over there, the wet grass lying slightly lower where he had previously trampled it; this being, surely, the path he had taken, and so, following the stamped grass like a woodland scout, he backtracked into the trees again, until he could see, thank God, the bike, on that uneven pile of leaves under which he had hidden the bags, and he raced over and threw the leaves off, and what happened next is a little bit cloudy, though you would think that it—this part, of all of it—would be the clearest of everything, as it was the real *beginning of the end*—the *moment of revelation*—but, strangely no; it isn't clear at all, and of course (of course), a story (or a memory) is not a transcript (quite obviously), or, if it is, if it is a transcript, then the stenographer would be drunk, the stenotype compromised, the jury bought, the lawyers incoherent, the testimony wildly biased; my point being that all of this is hazy, at best, some of it worse than that even, so bear with me, and continuing, here is what I see, as well as I can see it; bearing in mind that I cannot, now, even though I am taking great pains to conceal the fact, I cannot now see the face of even my red-haired girl, I have her contours, a few features, it is hard to admit, very hard (there are some things that, if I see them at all, it is through a kind of gauze; even her name comes to me muffled, as if said at a great distance), but there it is, and in any case the delivery boy rapidly brushed away the leaves, and then stood looking down at those four bags, pale and dirty and discolored yet still shining unhealthily in patches like a group of dubious mushrooms; these bags, his bags, his delivery, and considered everything for a beat, and, no other options forthcoming, tore into them with his fingers—his nails having grown long over his time in the warehouse—and he got through the first layer easily, and even, in places, punctured the second layer of plastic as well as the first, and could see then that the bags were, indeed, tripled, as he had suspected, those extra layers of shielding presaging something sinister; he didn't stop to consider this fully but kept tearing at the plastic until the first bag split its side, and (let us once more force an outcome via authorial mandate) out spilled, first, like an intestine, the single arm of what turned out to be a green wool sweater, which confused the delivery boy, who had to pause to consider its meaning before he pulled it out of the bag completely, and laid it, carefully, out upon the grass, at which point he turned back to the matter at hand and could see, in that same bag, more wool and cotton and the like, which, when he reached in and foal-ed it all out in a great big ball turned out to be: 1. A red hat. 2. Two flannel shirts, yellow and green. 3. Two pairs of trousers. 4. Some new socks. 5. Underwear. 6. A pair of gloves. 7. A scarf. Clothes, a hoard of clothes, which was beyond perplexing to the delivery boy and he racked his mind furiously as to why the Supervisor would ever need the delivery boy to deliver such nonsense, clothes of all things (it had no sense) and why, he wondered, would a mundane package like this one need to be transported in such strange, nefarious circumstances, and in what world could this, *this* even be considered an important delivery—a delivery so important as to negate the crime the delivery boy had committed—such a significant delivery as to necessitate urgency, secrecy, an almost mythical effort on the part of the deliverer, and worst of all by far to the delivery boy was this: that the contents of the bags were riddles, at least as puzzling as the bags themselves, meaning that there was no new information here, only more questions, new questions being the last thing the delivery boy wanted or needed, and so he dove forward, going directly at the second of the bags, going at it with increasing ferocity, clawing at the top, prying at the tight knots until the bag finally yielded, released, peeled open, and there it was: green, green, green; just bills, stacked and rubber-banded, a

sum the likes of which he had never seen before, a sum
that he couldn't entirely comprehend (the paltry amount
that my father had offered, desperately, to the officials at
our door—our entire savings—being literally laugh-
able by comparison, and I let out an involuntary little
huff just now, thinking of my father's naivete, that he
would ever be able to bribe those dark agents with such
an insulting amount, that sweet, deluded man—though
at least my father had been thinking on his feet, plot-
ting some alternative for us, while my mother raged
and reddened, contested and proselytized, rebutted,
shook her fists, always circling the future as if she were
to wrestle it down), while this money, this unthinkably
valuable pile here was at the very least confirmation of
the delivery boy's suspicions, i.e., it was almost exactly
what the delivery boy had been expecting from these
bags, that is, a delivery a sight more dangerous and
worth safeguarding than the bundle of garments (which
must have been, the delivery boy suspected, a feint, a
smuggler's trick, a magician's misdirection of some sort)
and so the delivery boy stared down at the newly opened
bag, a fortune spilling out of it, those bricks of bills, and
just gawked, eventually emerging from his daze to allow himself to contemplate sums, and rates, what things
cost, and how they are priced, meaning what his freedom, and N.'s might be worth, and gaming as best he
could a possible ending, which took some more time,

before remembering the precise nature of his predicament, and turning toward that third bag (and it is worth mentioning that, by this point, the delivery boy—though he still had no sense of what was in the last two bags, no inkling as to what was happening to him in the larger sense, no plan to follow, though he still felt so sunk inside a dark well of confusion, powerless in the face of his ever-diminishing options—he found himself feeling, counterintuitively, a bit calmer throughout this part of the episode, and in some sense he knew, as bad as things were, that he might as well slow down, breathe, that whatever path or paths were left to him, they could and must now be taken deliberately; though, of course, it may have been that his panic had reached such an intensity that that state, his preternatural calm, was actually shock), with a bit more care then, he picked up a stick, and poked at it, making a small, round indentation in it, which he began to worry, dilating the hole (and meanwhile, the sun had risen a bit further, some of the dew had begun burning off, and with the incipient warmth, the insects returned and he once again had to periodically swat at them, and there were moments when they formed a kind of thin veil around his face, which he would need to conduct away); but he kept working, kept pulling at the hole in the side of bag number three, and in this way eventually the aperture was wide enough to see into, and what he saw in there was a series of small cartons. He reached in and pulled one out, and it was a box of food, rice most likely, judging by the weight, and he ripped the sides of the bag open further, and there were more of them, like from one of those quick-food places; food. "Fuck," he said out loud to himself again, putting the flat of his hand up against one of the cartons, and, amazingly, he still felt some residual warmth emanate from inside of it, and the cramps in his stomach resumed immediately, there being little lag between his eyes and his gut, for he was truly starving, the exhaustion cutting through the nerves, but there was yet more to do, and, looking at the food containers, smelling them, and, most important, understanding their meaning, he felt himself ready now for final revelations, so, still unhurried, still kneeling, he pivoted over the remaining bag, clearing the remaining few leaves away, and, confident then of what he'd find, proceeded to open it; these knots giving way easily, and the contents revealed themselves . . . still, still: there were some real surprises left in that bag—in bag number four—for instance, among other things, he found (I'd wish to see) a brand-new power-assist, carefully wrapped and, even more surprising, the old, scalloped-edged photograph of N., slipped into the pages of the road map, the picture had fallen out of it, pitching in the breeze a few times, before landing, and the delivery boy picked it up from the ground and dusted it off and he saw three schoolchildren, and knew that one of them was N., and that the picture would have been taken back in those days before she was sent overseas, bought and sold into servitude to the Supervisor and warehouse, that the photo was taken back in the old country, and there was young N., sitting in the middle, wearing a simple costume, her hair up in a braided bun; on one side of her was a taller boy, and on the other side a smaller girl, who must have been a brother and a sister, judging by looks, all of them having the same broad cheekbones, wide-set eyes, and dark hair, all of their jawbones set in that truculent, defiant manner that the delivery boy had always considered a hallmark of N. (though now he could see that this was not just an adopted attitude of hers, a stance, a hard response to a hard world, but also a sign of her extraction, some ves-tige of what must have been the broad faces of her an-cestors, their character submerged and diluted, but phylogeny showing still, from many generations back, indelible in the family line), all of them looking stiff, if also brimming with a fierce pride, and the delivery boy stared at the photo for a while, wondering what it meant that she would give up such a cherished artifact to him, and after a period, finding what he concluded was the only satisfactory answer, he put the photo carefully into his breast pocket, examined the map again, searching until he found the spot where he now stood in real life (not difficult, as there was a large, handwritten red circle there, out of which emanated a thick red line, a line that ran a path from the orchard down to the river road, and then, from there, the line wound up, and up, zigzagging along with the river's knees and bends, meandering, but always moving, eventually, north, farther and farther north, this information too damning to consign to a phone, wishing there to be no trail lest the owner of the account were to search for it), and he nodded to himself, folding the map once more and tucking it away, after which, the how of it all being unknown to him, he conjured, in yet another disruption in the syntax of his own story, a series of new vignettes: of N., squirreling the money away bit by bit, as he himself had done; N., though, smarter, savvier, more furtive, patient, efficient, committing the same crime as his, but over a much longer period of time . . . unless, that is, the delivery boy considered, the money was taken all at once, brazenly, on the very night of the delivery boy's departure perhaps, when it was clear "how things stood," and she would have lifted the money from the safe in the back wall of the Supervisor's office, and the delivery boy then imagined a scenario in which N. built up trust over years, working her way inside, cozying up, the Supervisor eventually seeing in her, smart and unsentimental as she was, if not a willing partner, then a pliant one, but she would have been watching the Supervisor as well, and observed him putting away the take, seen him band it up night after night and stow it, late, after all the earnings were in and the delivery boys and dispatch girls were in their bunks; perhaps N. even counted the money for him (due to some educational or intellectual liability, the Supervisor might have needed someone to do this) and so N. could have studied his routine—how he'd sweep up the bills into a bag, and then amble over to the safe, turn the dial, and she'd pick up bits of the combination over time, one number at a time, by following his movements, or hearing and counting those clicks, or perhaps she got this information out of, say, Uncle, or perhaps the Supervisor had simply *told* her (and the delivery boy did not want to imagine how this particular narrative could have ever come to pass; meaning that the delivery boy avoided imagining what N. would have had to do, what unfathomable debasements might have been necessary to induce such trust and intimacy in such a man), and each scene that played out in the delivery boy's mind, each explanation— plausible to implausible—for the illicit bounty that N. (and I) had prepared for him ended with the same conclusion, and the delivery boy was reminded, with each of these possible storylines, of the danger she had faced, the extent of her courage, and stunned by a commingling of shame and admiration, yet not, in fact able to bear or fathom such sacrifice, the delivery boy turned away—and returned to that final bag, limp on the ground, which he shook, to make sure there was in fact nothing hidden there, nothing left inside, because he absolutely *knew* at this point that there was one thing left to find, one thing left unresolved, a final clue, and he saw something stuck to the bottom of the plastic, so he reached in and pulled out what turned out to be a single, creased sheet of paper, which he read with an almost occult concentration; read what was written there (*I am gone now, if you come back you will not find me . . .*), taking in every last word, reading it over and over again, until he was sure he understood everything, every manner in which the letter could be understood, in all its various nuances, on each of its channels of meaning, until he had it memorized, until he could (and did) speak the letter out loud to himself, beginning to end, and, satisfied then, he carefully closed it up, slid it in next to the photograph in his breast pocket, buttoning it up so nothing could fall out, and then bent down, and began to mend the torn bags as best he could: he put the clothes back away—though first exchanging his wet socks for a fresh pair—and bundled up the money; tied up the ragged ends of the bags, and then . . .

. . . then the next thing is an image, a single scene only, discrete and disconnected; an unexpected clause in which the delivery boy is sitting in a small tree-lined alcove on the cliff face, a kind of natural loge from

which he overlooks the drama of the river below; his
legs are crossed out in front of him, his back leaning up
against a trunk, and he seems, in this picture, in this
tableau: relaxed, content; he is eating, dipping in and
out of one of those food containers, looking for all the
world as if he were finally at his leisure; the food warms
him, fills him up, the view of the snaking river beneath
him lights up his eyes, and in this scene he periodically
stops eating to wipe his mouth with a thin paper napkin, which is soon covered in as much road dirt as it is
food, and he eats and eats, scans the waterway, yawns,
and belches, and reclines fully, and in this scene he
finds himself drifting off once again, though this time
dreamlessly, into a light doze, a pleasant hiatus from his
odyssey, this journey that was, in fact, just another leg of
an even longer one, as if his original point of debarka-
tion were drifting away and backward on an ebb tide of
history, and I see the delivery boy, there in his repose,
how he remained there, until the sun found him beneath those apple branches, shone on him directly, scin-
tillating on his lashes, suffusing his head, and after a
period, a period in which the delivery boy mulled over
his new, hard-won knowledge——he understood at long
last the language that N. was speaking to him through
this, her final dispatch, and finding himself capable of
this understanding, having gained this new faculty, he
further found himself staggered by it, staring, unfo-

cused out at the wall of green trees (and I can see my father's green banker's lamp casting its nebula over the far wall of his study at night, and the sunlight catching the faded yellow cover of my school notebook, and the red glow of neon from the café across from our old apartment . . . that red glow, red glow, and, suddenly, so clear to me now also, this red synonymous with another, there she is, blushing in that delicate space on her neck, the dark red hairs, tucked behind her ear, whorled about it, the finer, lighter hairs beneath those; and I see the minute mark she bore below her left eye like the faint tattoo of a pencil tip, her scent bridging the remove between us . . . bergamot, lemon . . . her mouth, pursed wryly in anticipatory wit, her lip rising on one side only, hovering there shakily like a tethered balloon, this wry look of hers that might detonate into laughter but could also dispel itself in modest fashion, with a small puff of air, attended by a kind of Gallic shrug, and when she spoke, her untamed sentences galloped down forking bridle paths that I breathlessly tried to navigate, all those thoughts tumbling out, this her red-faced enthusiasm but God help me, her temper, her bright red fury— but it was her pride-red admiration I wanted to earn, more than any prize yet on offer upon the gaudy shelves of adolescence's carnival booths, after the kiss most of all, which had been quick, presumably, if measured in the unimpeachable time of gears and springs, but re-

277

membering that after our bodies parted she had turned to go into her apartment without looking back, and I had stood there a moment, then stumbled out the green door, down and out, under the yellow streetlamps, modulating through the streets, the embrace replaying itself over and over, as the road took me down another hill, and I found myself out on the banks, alone with the night, and the night birds, and the sound of the river beside me, and the sweet air—down from the mountains—and as I lay there, facing the sky, the moon rose, and life spoke a kind of gibberish) and so it took the delivery boy some time, staring at that river, and out beyond it, before he was able to finally rock himself up to his feet, and once standing, wipe his mouth one last time, shoving the used napkin into a pocket before he walked over to his bicycle, picked it up off the ground, then, crouching, pried the old and bent power-assist motor off the frame, tossing it aside into a nearby bush, and attached the new one, which was easy, as it snapped right into place, and revved beautifully upon being activated; flicking it off again, he stood and wheeled the bicycle out and away from the tree trunks, loaded up the newly consolidated bags on the rear rack, strapping them down tightly with all his bungee cords, and when all this was complete, he put his kickstand up, and guided the once-again laden bicycle back down the hill, carefully maneuvering it over roots, carrying it on his shoulders over the steeper inclines, weaving in and out of the rocks, not pausing for breath, working his way back down until he saw that fallen log that marked the end of the orchard road, and he patted the dirt off his behind, zipped up his jacket, rolled up his sleeves, mounted the bike, put his right foot on a raised pedal, straightened his arms on the handlebars locking his elbows, and leaned forward; and with that began, once again, to ride—this being the last time he would need to retrace his steps, those moments in which he returned over his bike's tire marks from the prior evening, but when he reached the beginning of the pavement again, yet another leave-taking (*mutatis mutandis* I am on that quay with the smell of the sea, stenched with petrol, and the seabirds and the crowds and the slow, unsteady dipping of one skyline—a skyline of wheelhouses, smokestacks, masts—facing off against the rooted wall of buildings at my back, all of us—migrants, refugees—a teeming mass of people shuffling forward toward the piers—the final vestiges of land, like the shore's long arms, stretched out for one last attempt to push us off, or grab us back—the birds pleading, joining in with the long whines of the vessel's fenders, rubbing up forcefully against the stone docks, and the loud snapping of sails and clanking of chains, the shrill blasts from steam pipes, the shouts of sailors and longshoremen, and the brute anxiety, our mob heaving along, but everyone stuck, ultimately, in place, the sheer volume of people causing an intractable jam, the boats, which were so close, so close, being our salvation, presumably, yet also the inauguration of something terrifying and new as well: an exit—perhaps equally fearsome to the more certain fears we faced back on land—all of us, children, adults, elderly pressed together into rough lines that joined, and split, and rejoined again, the gull-beseeched throng pushing toward gangplanks, some pushing carts, hauling with us a life's worth of possessions, most bearing nothing at all, with the wave-whipped air breeching our worn-out coats, headscarves, threadbare trousers; me, gripping her thin little hand as tightly as I am able, but still, with the surging crowd, tiding around us . . .), but this time the delivery boy turned left and away, turned away from the city, and his past, and toward altogether new scenes, hugging the shoulder of the road as it wound through the countryside, down one hill after another, and only a single car or two passed by him, as it was true woodland out there; perhaps, he thought, the beginnings of the national park he had noticed—a large geometric block of green on N.'s map—and, as it was so early, no one was awake except the delivery boy and the birds, who trilled noisily over-head, and the sun kept tapping him on the shoulder, and the bike sailed on, smooth, no more noise or com-plaint, no need for power assistance or even pedaling, as the road was diving, ineluctably toward the waterway and thus low, flat ground, and as he was completely free from exertion, he felt disembodied—part of the bicycle—and he did nothing at all but listen to the sound of the wind skimming by him, did not even think about (though he knew, he knew that this could, and perhaps should be the time for a final reminiscence before turning forever forward—a final memory of home perhaps, of lost, true homes, last, fond glances back at mothers and fathers, brothers . . . unintentionally final, parting words one can't bear reprising, or more general recollections of love, of deep tenderness—or a parting image of the girl with the French horn, a thought for her plight but, more important, for her, her selfhood, now lost, the extinction of yet one more of time's prodigies, and perhaps, therefore, a final romantic episode recalled, maybe one in which they gazed at each other, or sat, merely adjacent, in each other's orbit, in her parents' garret apartment, in their seats in the rehearsal hall, out in the rough and shining fields of those rally days, or on the slick white marble floor of the old public hall, on that once-and-forever-conclusive occasion before the place was shuttered and all the dances canceled, when we can imagine the delivery boy extending a hand, bidden by a secretive and fugitive force, thinking then that, more surprising still how the hand would be taken up, gently, and he would escort the girl with the French horn, both

281

of them bewildered by their own behavior, out into the crowd, aqueous lights drifting around them, and they would sway in place, neither leading, both led) and though this would be the truly proper occasion to leave them, there, though again maybe this moment may call for a recapitulation of another sort, for some other, more minor curtain call, for instance, one for the conductor, who deserves, perhaps, some kind of callback, whether for that yellow coat, which was never really yellow, but which, there on the bike, on the road, as the delivery boy flew headlong down the hills of Manor Grove, in the onrush of his new articulacy, he recognized as taupe, fawn, honey, muslin, eggshell, ivory (it had been khaki, and her hair had not been red—not the red of signs, brake lights, and stop signals, but auburn—and her eyes were brown), or for the conductor's sophistication and culture, which stood in stark contrast to that general collective barbarity that would come later down the road, an upheaval that is often only a little ways around a curve, any curve, danger and death over the rise (but not here—not while I am steering—and I would deliver him, at the very least, into ambiguity), or perhaps then a concluding anecdote about the power of music itself, that medium that the conductor embodied and signified; say, a word in particular about musical conclusions, percussive tonic chords, final cymbal clashes, maudlin, insistent (endings I dislike immensely, being of a particularly subjunctive disposition), or a word or two in favor of its movement, its carving out duration from the diffuse flux of time's momentum, its reliance on the accumulation of memory, the buildup of it, and thus each and every work's nostalgia for its own simple beginnings, its more naive idioms, and yet, yet: what would be the point here now, as forward motion is precisely the point, forward motion being what it means to endure, what endurance requires—the ability *to go on*, to pedal, to set one's eyes upriver, and so that is what he did then, meaning that the delivery boy did not spare a thought for his memories, and the cast that populated these memories, but rather, determined to make the northern road by the time the sun had crested the cliffs on the far side of the water, he leaned forward, making himself small and aerodynamic, and the bike flew and the air whipped about him, and he squinted his eyes into the wind, leaning into the coming curves, humming a song, an old one, humming it to himself, flying under the swift ledger lines overhead, the dew-hung, web-strung stalks beside the road, beside his thrumming bike, flashing in the early sun, until finally the road bottomed out, and he swung in a wide arc to his right, and onto a small, two-lane street, and he knew he was there; meaning that he had arrived then at the river road, at last, and he took it, and the river stretched out to his left, wider than he had imagined it and a barge

somewhere upriver blared its throaty horn as if in wel-
come and he put his feet back down on the pedals and
began once again to work, though it felt as natural as
breathing and he followed the road and therefore the
river followed it out and away from the city and the
tight ambit of his previously bonded life, and he could
see, following its lines and currents, that as if via some
application of narrative magic, the estuary had reversed
its flow, now following him upriver and away, and he
recognized then, as I do, a capacity for moving forward,
an ability to go on endlessly if necessary, on and on, and
though he did not yet know what he was moving toward
he knew then that a happy life was a headlong life and
a fluent life and that whatever was to befall him at
the end, he would be able to say, finally, that he was
conversant.

AUTHOR'S NOTE

The three epigraphs opening the three sections of this book are taken from *Philosophical Investigations*, third edition, by Ludwig Wittgenstein, translated by G. E. M. Anscombe.

—I§18. "Our language can be seen as an ancient city: a maze of little streets and squares, of old and new houses, and of houses with additions from various periods; and this surrounded by a multitude of new boroughs with straight regular streets . . ."

—I§691. "When I make myself a sketch of N.'s face from memory, I can surely be said to mean, by my drawing: [her]."

—I§179. "We can also imagine the case where nothing at all occurred in one's mind except that one suddenly said 'Now I know how to go on.'"

ACKNOWLEDGMENTS

The author would like to thank: J.M.D., S.M., L.S., M.A., F.C., C.P.L., S.K., B.K., O.M., M.T., D.S., A.M., D.G., M.W., R.V.K., S.O., C.H., J.M.

Peter Mendelsund is a novelist, a graphic designer, and the creative director of *The Atlantic*. He is the author of three books about literature and the visual imagination: *What We See When We Read*, *Cover*, and *The Look of the Book: Jackets, Covers, and Art at the Edges of Literature*. His debut novel, *Same Same*, was published in 2019.